SAUERKRAUT

Also by Kelly Jones

Unusual Chickens for the Exceptional Poultry Farmer

Are You Ready to Hatch an Unusual Chicken?

Murder, Magic, and What We Wore

SAUERKRAUT

BY KELLY JONES

illustrated by Paul Davey

Alfred A. Knopf

New York

For Mom and Dad,
who never said no to a project,
and for makers everywhere

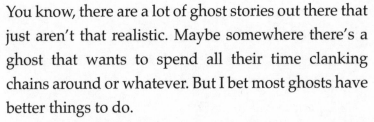

1

You know, there are a lot of ghost stories out there that just aren't that realistic. Maybe somewhere there's a ghost that wants to spend all their time clanking chains around or whatever. But I bet most ghosts have better things to do.

They're busy people, after all, and they're pretty focused on what they need to do.

Kind of like me. Only, more ghostly.

My full name is Hans Dieter Schenk. My dad's name is Hans Peter Schenk. Before him came Hans Gerhard

Schenk, and before that came Hans Franz Schenk. (He wanted to be called Franz, because, come on, would you introduce yourself as Hans Franz? It would not be good, not even in olden times.) Before him came more guys back in Germany called Hans Something too. They all looked pretty much the same in old photos, with pale skin and pale hair and square chins and eyes that were probably blue, like my dad's. All except for Hans Franz, who had a bigger nose than the rest.

They all fit their names exactly.

Mom says I got my chin from my dad. But honestly, I look a lot more like her and my little brother, Asad. I have short black locs, and medium-brown skin, and brown eyes, and no one ever thinks my dad is my dad unless they know us. (Sometimes they even think my dad is my best friend Eli's dad, not mine, just because they're both white. It's . . . awkward.)

So, people call me HD.

My mom's name is Kikora Davis Schenk. She has darker skin than me and much longer locs, and she is a no-nonsense person. She says that knowing where you came from is important, but so is knowing who you are, and what kind of person you want to become.

I've been thinking about that a lot lately.

Right now, most adults know me as "Kikora's son— the older one" (because everybody knows my mom) or "Hans Peter's son—the older one," or "Gregor's oldest nephew," or "that boy who takes care of Mr. Ziedrich's goats for him." Most kids know me as "that Black kid with the white dad and the weird name—the older one," or even "Asad's older brother."

But after they've seen the computer I'm going to build from scratch, old-school-style, they'll know me as "HD, the maker."

I like the sound of that.

HD'S COMPUTER BUILD:

TO BUY:

COMPONENTS:

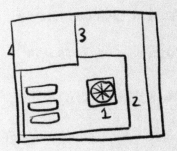

CPU (Central Processing Unit): computes stuff. A fan keeps it from overheating.

Motherboard: connects everything together and sends power to the other components.

Memory, aka RAM (random-access memory): helps the computer remember what it's doing while it's working on something.

Storage (a hard disk drive or solid-state drive): stores all the software and files that you save on the computer.

Power supply: gets the right amount of electricity to the computer.

Case: keeps the dust out of your components and has a power button and ports for peripherals.

PERIPHERALS:

Monitor: the screen.

Keyboard: what you type on.

Mouse: what you click with.

HOW MUCH IT WILL COST:

At least $300, even if I shop carefully and buy used peripherals.

I've been saving all year, but I only have $50.23. I want to enter my computer into the county fair, and that's less than a month away.

I was supposed to go to tech camp in Seattle with Eli. We'd been looking forward to it all year, learning how to build cool stuff, even if we couldn't take it home afterward. But I guess they let some science get totally out of hand, and their lab burned down, so they had to cancel camp. By then, the other tech camps in our area were full.

I was really disappointed. But Mr. Z. said he'd teach me how to build my own computer, and Dad and Uncle Gregor came up with a plan so I could earn enough for everything I'd need. All I have to do is go through all the stuff in Uncle Gregor's basement.

See, when Grandma Schenk died a few years ago, Uncle Gregor went to Arizona to sort stuff out and sell her house. But it turned out she had a LOT of stuff, and he didn't have much time, so he brought it all back in a truck and put it in his basement. He's been busy, and looking at her stuff makes him pretty sad.

So, since Uncle Gregor's away this summer and I'm good at figuring out what somebody can use and what's just trash, he and Dad decided this would be a good summer job for me.

There are more than fifty boxes of stuff in Uncle Gregor's basement. But Uncle Gregor left $250 in an envelope with my name on it, for when I'm done.

That's some serious motivation.

2

Eli and I went to check out Uncle Gregor's basement and make a plan after school.

Eli peered down the dark steps into Uncle Gregor's crowded, gloomy basement and shivered. "Creepy."

I flipped the light switch on, but one bare bulb didn't light it all up. "It's just a basement full of stuff. We wouldn't be nervous at all if we hadn't watched so many monster movies last weekend."

"I bet there's a chain-saw murderer over there," Eli said, pointing. "Look, he even left his chain saw where he can grab it when he jumps out at us."

"That's Uncle Gregor's old chain saw," I told Eli. "It probably ran out of gas years ago. Besides, if anyone was down here, he wouldn't be standing around while we argued."

Eli crossed his arms. "Then what are you waiting for?"

The hair on my arms was standing up by then, but I wasn't going to tell Eli that. I took a step down the narrow stairs, and then another.

No one jumped out from the shadows.

I hopped down the last few steps and yanked on the string attached to the main light. It came on. No monsters, no murderers, just lots of boxes of Grandma Schenk's stuff. "See? No one's here," I said. I opened the lid of the first box, lifted a big brown pottery jar out of it, and set it down on Uncle Gregor's workbench. I blew off the dust, and sneezed.

"Who are you?" said a voice right next to my ear.

A voice that was not Eli, because he was still standing at the top of the basement stairs.

A voice that told me someone else actually *was* in the basement with us.

If I always ran as fast as I did up those stairs, I would be the new middle school track champion, for sure.

Eli ran, but I glanced back through the basement door. Whoever was there had been right next to me. But I couldn't see anyone. Only . . . was the air . . . moving?

We ran through Uncle Gregor's front door and out into the sun, gasping.

"Did you see who was down there?" I asked, breathing hard.

"I saw you freak out and run up the stairs yelling!" Eli said.

"But you heard it, right?" Maybe Eli would know what to do next. I hadn't seen as many horror movies as him.

"All I heard was you screaming!" Eli said, frowning.

"Before all that—you didn't hear anyone else?" I asked.

He shook his head.

It didn't make sense. That question was loud, and Eli has very good hearing. "I thought I heard something," I said.

Eli stared at me. "You ran screaming up the stairs because you thought you heard something? You said you weren't even scared to go down there and I was just making stuff up!" Then he took a step back. "I didn't make stuff up. You did. You tried to fool me, to scare me."

Then he picked up his helmet and got on his bike without another word.

"Did not!" I said. I know Eli really hates it when

people try to prank him. I thought he knew I'd never do that to him. And definitely not like this.

"I didn't hear anyone. You weren't that far away, and I didn't see anyone there."

"There's something freaky down there!" I said. "Really!"

Eli didn't look scared anymore. He looked mad. "Tell someone else. I'm going home." He started pedaling.

I looked at my bike. There was no point in following him. Eli wasn't going to talk about it anymore without proof I wasn't pranking him.

I could have gone home too, I guess. I could have come back later with my mom and dad. But now I was starting to doubt myself. Maybe there actually wasn't anyone there at all?

I stood in Uncle Gregor's hallway for a long time, and I listened very carefully. I wasn't stupid. I was ready to run if someone was down there.

But I didn't hear anything at all.

So I peeked through the basement door. I didn't see anyone. Both lights were still on, and everything looked the same as before.

But I couldn't make my foot take the first step down the stairs.

And then I saw the air move again. It was like a cloud of thick air was hovering over the big brown pottery jar. I stared. What could it be?

As I stared, I heard the question again. "Who are you?" It was coming from the thick air.

I already know that when people find out that the world is bigger and more complicated than they thought—like when they meet an alien for the first time, or discover they have a superpower—they have to make a choice. Are they going to let fear make them do stupid stuff and turn them into a supervillain, like Lex Luthor? Or are they going to figure out what's really going on first, so they can act appropriately, like Kamala Khan and the Men in Black?

I spend a lot of time thinking about this stuff. If you asked me yesterday, I would have told you, sure, I was ready to deal with whatever came my way.

But today something weird happened, and instead of dealing with it, I freaked out and ran, even though I know better.

So I was still scared, but I was also determined: that's not who I want to be. Okay. Think. What did I observe?

I still couldn't see any other people down there,

only that thick air. The thick air that was moving very slowly toward me now, and growing larger, and larger.

"Who are you?" it asked again.

This time, I paid attention. The voice was definitely coming from the thick air. And the voice didn't sound like a chain-saw murderer or a scary clown.

Actually, it sounded kind of like my Grandma Schenk.

I hadn't seen my Grandma Schenk since I was a little kid. And I have to admit, when I used to play Black Panther, and ask my ancestors to help me out, I never thought any of the Schenks would show up. But ancestors are ancestors, and besides, my parents raised me to be polite.

So, I answered. "I'm Hans Dieter Schenk, but everyone calls me HD. Who—or what—are you?"

The thick air was coming up the stairs. I wondered if I should run now and try again later.

But what if I was the only person in the world who had ever met someone like this? What if the world depended on me hearing what it had to say? That stuff happens in comics all the time. I stared at the thick air and reminded myself that sometimes superheroes look just as strange to us as supervillains do.

The thick air rushed up the stairs and swirled

around me, so close it brushed my locs. It stopped and said, "Hans Dieter. Are you Hans Gerhard's son?"

"No, I'm Hans Peter's son," I told it. "Hans Gerhard was my granddad. Who are you?"

"Hans Gerhard is my grandson," the thick air replied.

Whoa. Definitely an ancestor.

It whooshed forward.

I flinched, but the thick air didn't hurt me. It—well—it kind of kissed me on the cheek, I think.

"He died before I was born," I told it.

The thick air made a funny noise, kind of like a cough, or someone about to cry. It whooshed back down the stairs, curled around that brown jar, and flowed inside.

"Are you okay?" I thought ancestors were supposed to already know who else had passed on.

But nothing came out of the jar, and nobody answered.

"I'm sorry if you're sad," I told the jar. I watched it for a minute longer, to make sure it wasn't going to explode or have a lot more ancestors come out of it or anything. It didn't. "Uh, bye for now," I said.

Then I stepped back into the hallway, shut the door, and sat down with my back against it while I decided a few things:

1. I really had talked to some thick air that said my grandfather was its grandson. Since it sounded like a lady, it was probably my great-great-grandmother. And since my great-great-grandmothers had been dead a long time, and I wasn't actually the Black Panther, she was probably a ghost.

2. I wasn't making things up, and I probably wasn't crazy. If I was going to make up a ghost, it would look much cooler than that. And I already know that there's no point wasting a lot of time wondering if things are real just when they start getting interesting. If real life starts to seem weird, it's probably because sometimes real life is weird.

3. I needed to find someone I could talk to about this. Like Agent J has Agent K, and Elastigirl has that lady who hates capes. Someone who helps them learn what they need to know, and focus on what needs to be done. Grandpop Davis always says that most of the world's problems would be solved if people would take time to hear

each other and work together to solve things. So I just needed to figure out who might believe me.

Eli is my best friend, and he's good at figuring things out. But he was mad at me. My parents were at work, and I wasn't sure whether a ghost who didn't seem to be hurting anyone counted as an emergency. So I decided to go talk to Mr. Ziedrich, since it was time to take the goats to visit him anyway.

I got up, walked very quickly out of Uncle Gregor's house, locked the front door, and rode my bike home to get the goats.

3

The goats' names are Rodgers and Hammerstein. They belong to my friend Mr. Ziedrich, but I take care of them for him now. They moved into a shed in our backyard when Mr. Z. moved into Maple Falls last year. After his wife died, he decided he was ready to get some help with the things his fingers didn't want to do anymore, and to spend more time with people his own age, but he felt bad that Rodgers and Hammerstein couldn't come with him.

So my parents decided I was old enough and responsible enough to come home after school to take care of the goats and walk them over to see Mr. Z. and check in with him, instead of going to Dad and Uncle

Gregor's auto body shop like Asad. And in return, Mr. Z. is helping me build some cool stuff, like my computer.

Taking care of goats is a lot of work. I have to make sure they have food and water and salt, and clean out their shed, and make sure nothing poisonous is growing where they can eat it, and that they don't need their hooves trimmed again. But I would miss those silly guys if they went to live somewhere else.

Besides, Mr. Z. has been helping me figure out how to make things for years, and I like helping him out for a change. And even though the auto body shop is fine, I'm glad I'm old enough to do my own thing now. Especially since Asad still has to go hang out with Dad. Sometimes I need a break from my little brother.

As soon as I let myself into the backyard, Rodgers started chewing on the hay-loader rope, which he knows he's not supposed to do. And then Hammerstein pooped right in the salt lick.

Gross.

But it's hard to be mad at goats for long. Hammerstein jumped up on the roof of their playhouse and grinned at me, and Rodgers jumped all around the goat-proof treat box, to give me a hint about what I should do next, and I had to laugh. And then

Hammerstein jumped down and came to say hi, so I had to pet him at least a little.

I took the goat-proof treat box away from Rodgers, gave him a scratch on the chin instead of a treat, and dumped out the poopy salt. Then I refilled the salt, and double-checked that there was still hay in the manger.

I knew the goats were ready for a walk because they let me put their collars on instead of playing chase.

It took me a while to learn to walk goats. They'd never gone for a walk when they lived with Mr. and Mrs. Z., so they freaked out about collars and leashes and almost broke my arm trying to charge the ice cream truck once. But it got easier after they decided I was part of their herd. They let me lead the way as long as they got to stop and eat whatever looked interesting.

So off we went, in our usual routine of jogging, zigzagging, and waiting around while they ate leaves. It's a good thing Maple Falls is only a few blocks away.

I was glad to see Mr. Z. sitting in his chair on the patio. The first time I brought Rodgers and Hammerstein to Maple Falls, a lady who worked there thought I was some kind of vandal and started yelling at me, just for being there. Maybe because I'm a Black kid, or maybe not. I don't really know. Then Mr. Z. came back from the bathroom, and I've never seen anything like it. I could have explained all day long and that lady wouldn't have listened to a word I said, but Mr. Z. opened his mouth and rolled right over her issues. Before you knew it, she'd agreed that I could come whenever I wanted, and I didn't even have to clean up the goat poop. He told me if I ever had an experience like that again there, to let him know right away, because he did not want his friends treated like that. If Mr. Z.'s secret ability is convincing people like he did then, it's a good thing he's on our side.

I waved at Mr. Z., and brought the goats over to say hi. I could tell they missed him.

Mr. Z. patted Hammerstein's head and scratched Rodgers's chin. *"Hallo, HD. Wie geht's dir?"*

That means "Hello, HD. How are you?" Mr. Z. has been teaching me German since he found out I didn't know any, even though I'm half–German American. Grandmom and Grandpop Davis and Aunt Nia take me and Asad to learn about Black culture at museums and festivals and stuff every time we visit. There aren't that many other Black people where we live, but we know our roots on Mom's side. Grandma and Grandpa Schenk didn't teach Dad and Uncle Gregor about their roots, though. So Mom and Dad and I decided Mr. Z. could help me out with that part, since he's from Germany.

"Es geht mir gut," I said. *"Ich habe etwas Neues gelernt."* (That means "I'm pretty good. I have learned something new." That's a phrase I use a lot, since I'm always learning new things, and Mr. Z. is always interested in them.)

"Ah!" Mr. Z.'s bushy white eyebrows rose way up. "And what have you learned this time?"

I hesitated. Mr. Z. doesn't read comics. Maybe he wouldn't understand.

But ever since we became friends, I'd always told Mr. Z. what I was working on, and sometimes, when I got stuck, he had ideas that helped.

I took a deep breath. "I learned that there's a ghost in Uncle Gregor's basement."

Mr. Z.'s eyebrows shot up even further. For a minute he looked startled, and maybe sad?

Then his eyebrows settled down. "Indeed.... What brings you to this conclusion?"

The goats' leads felt slippery. I moved them to my other hand. I didn't need to worry about chasing any goats right now. "Well, when Eli and I went down

there, someone asked me who I was. But I couldn't see anyone there, and Eli didn't hear it."

Mr. Z. nodded slowly. "Sometimes we hear things we do not expect. But often there is an explanation for it."

"What else would sound like my Grandma Schenk?" I asked.

Mr. Z. shrugged. "There are many unexpected sounds in old basements—something tapping on a furnace duct, or brushing against a window in the wind. You were looking at her things, perhaps missing her—the brain is very powerful, and it can play tricks on us. Even scientists like you and me."

I didn't think so. But it was too hard to explain that I didn't really know Grandma Schenk well enough to miss her, or about the ghost not being her after all, but actually my great-great-grandma, who I'd never met.

Mr. Z. studied my face, then smiled. "You always do your research, HD. I know you will look into this new topic, and learn something valuable." He nudged Rodgers's front feet off of his chair before Rodgers could climb all the way up on it. "In fact, there's someone you should meet—someone who might help you with this research."

As I watched him unfold his creaky bones from his chair, I stopped being mad at him. (He doesn't like me to offer to pull him up, even though it's what any friend would do.) Maybe Mr. Z. didn't believe what I heard. But he would still try to help me.

"Really?" I asked as the goats and I followed him down the path that leads around Maple Falls. "Who?"

"Someone who is visiting a friend of mine today," he answered, leading me toward a small patio with two chairs under one of those big outside umbrellas.

An older white lady with curly white hair was asleep in one of them. The other white lady was awake. She had reddish hair, and she nodded at us, and examined the goats.

"Good afternoon, Ms. Stevermer," Mr. Z. said. "This is my friend HD, and my goats, Rodgers and Hammerstein. HD is researching a new project in your area of expertise. I wondered if you might be able to answer any questions he has."

Ms. Stevermer made a note in the small notebook in her lap. She tipped her head, and examined me through her glasses. "Certainly, I would be happy to."

Mr. Z.'s watch alarm beeped. He hesitated.

"Movie matinee?" I asked him. Mr. Z. has a very busy schedule.

"No, today I play pool with Mr. Slater," he said. "You are welcome to join us, of course."

I shook my head. Mr. Slater doesn't like any noises

while he's playing pool, and it's hard to keep the goats quiet, even if we wait on the lawn outside. "You go ahead," I told him. "I'm fine."

Mr. Z. nodded. *"Bis bald,"* he said, giving Rodgers and Hammerstein a final pat. (That means "See you soon.")

"Tschüss," I said. (That means "bye.")

Mr. Z. walked slowly back along the path toward the pool hall.

"It's not very often that my expertise is called upon. How can I help?" Ms. Stevermer asked.

"What's your area of expertise?" I didn't want to talk about different kinds of furnace noises all afternoon.

"I'm a writer," Ms. Stevermer told me. "I write and collect ghost stories."

I blinked. "Really?"

"Yes, really. Let's see, now—since my mother is asleep in that chair, would you like me to call the staff for another one?"

"Thanks, but I'm good," I said. "It's better if I keep the goats away from chairs, and anything else they can climb on."

"Very sensible," she said. "Now, was there something you wanted to ask me about?"

I am a matter-of-fact person, but this wasn't easy

stuff to talk about. But Grandpop Davis always says to go ahead and tell people what's on your mind, if you have the energy, because even if they can't hear it or believe you right then, maybe they'll remember it later.

I cleared my throat. "So, I'm sorting out my grandma's stuff for my dad and my uncle, because she died, and no one's gone through it yet." I snuck a glance at the writer, and she was nodding. So far so good. "I took this big brown jar out of a box in the basement—"

"Glass?" Ms. Stevermer asked.

"What?" I asked.

"Is it a glass jar?" she asked.

"No, it's a pottery one, I think."

"Tall and skinny, or short and stout?"

I thought back. "About a foot and a half tall, and about a foot wide, maybe, with handles on the sides."

She was nodding again, making notes in her notebook. "A pickling crock, then."

Huh. Maybe she could help me after all. "I think it's haunted by my great-great-grandmother. I can't exactly see her, but she came out to talk to me."

She nodded, still making notes. "All pickling crocks are haunted."

"All of them?" I asked. "Why are they haunted?"

"Well, all the old ones that are left, anyway. I haven't

made a study of the new ones yet. Butter churns never are." Ms. Stevermer didn't look the slightest bit startled. "As for why, I intend to find out. What did your great-great-grandmother have to say about it?"

Yeah, this writer was tough. No way was she going to freak out over a ghost like my great-great-grandmother. "She didn't say all that much, really. Just that my granddad was her grandson. She seemed sad when I told her he died a long time ago."

She nodded. "Time doesn't seem to pass the same way for ghosts as it does for the rest of us. They aren't always very good at sticking to relevant topics either."

"Have you met a lot of ghosts?" I asked.

"No, none yet," she said calmly. "I've read lots of reports, though."

"Then maybe you could—I mean—would you mind just, you know, checking her out, to make sure she's safe or whatever?"

She looked up from her notes and smiled at me. "I'd love to meet your great-great-grandmother, but ghosts don't appear to everyone. I've tried many times, but I haven't had your luck."

I sighed. "Is there anything I should do about her?"

"Oh, no, I don't think so. Don't let her take over your body or make you try to hurt anyone, obviously.

That's pretty rare, though. As long as you don't break her crock or try to exorcise her, you should do fine."

I guess she saw from my face that I wasn't so sure of that.

"Ghosts aren't here to bother anyone who's never done anything to them," she told me. "Usually they have a job they need to do—their Grand Purpose, they call it in the literature—and when it's done, they continue on. Perhaps you can help your great-great-grandmother with hers."

Hammerstein put his hoof up on the arm of the writer's chair, so I lured him away with a dandelion, and thought about that. Aside from startling me, my ghost didn't seem so bad. And I was already helping Uncle Gregor out with a job. Maybe I could help the ghost out with hers too.

"Anything else?" the writer asked me.

I hesitated. Rodgers and Hammerstein were getting antsy and starting to head-butt each other. But I needed to know. "Do you think I'm crazy?"

She examined me, then shook her head. "I'm sure you already know that not every ghostly appearance turns out to be supernatural, just like not every bright light in the sky is an alien spaceship. But you seem like an observant young man, so I have no doubt that you heard something, and that you'll continue your observations until you've learned everything you can. If you do thorough research, and question everything, that will see you through."

Research. I knew plenty about that. "Thanks," I told her.

She smiled at me. "Of course. I do hope you tell me what you learn."

"I'll do that," I said.

I was going to tell Mom and Dad what happened at dinner that night. But somehow, when it was my turn, instead of telling them I met a ghost, I said, "Eli probably doesn't want to come stay with us while his mom is on her trip anymore. We had a fight today." I looked down at my plate. We'd been making a list of every fun thing we were going to do ever since we found out camp was canceled and Eli was coming here for almost a month instead. Now I might as well rip that list up.

"Oh, sweetie," Mom said, and she got up to give me a hug. "What happened? Something you want me to talk to his mom about?"

"Nah, it's not a Black thing," I told her. "He thought I was trying to fool him about—something," I said.

My throat felt tight, and I didn't have the energy to force all those words out. "I told him I wasn't, but he didn't believe me. He just left."

She gave me another squeeze. "You know, even good friends can go through rough times. But I bet you can still work things out."

Dad nodded. "Sometimes guys need a little time to cool down and realize they're wrong. Eli's a pretty smart guy. I bet he'll figure it out soon. And you're a pretty smart guy too. Maybe you can explain your side to him in a different way."

Maybe. I nodded, and my stomach finally got hungry enough for Dad's sloppy joes. But when I thought about telling them about the ghost, my stomach started to hurt again. So I didn't.

Not yet.

4

The next morning, I woke up with a bad feeling. I stared at my posters and tried to think why. Miles Morales in his Spider-Verse suit, astronaut Leland Melvin with his dogs, the patent drawing for Lonnie Johnson's Super Soaker, the Black Panther and Shuri, some Maker Faire Africa art that looked straight out of Wakanda. . . . Usually they remind me I can do whatever I put my mind to. And today was the last day of school, and then Eli was coming to stay with us tonight—oh. Yeah.

I knew his mom couldn't cancel her work trip, or she would have when our tech camp got canceled. So Eli probably had to come stay with us. But if we didn't stop fighting, this was going to be the worst summer ever, instead of the best.

So while I got ready for school, I made a plan. Plans are the only way you can make complex stuff happen. I mean, you don't just wake up one morning and build a space station before dinner.

First I decided what my goals were.

1. To convince Eli to stop being mad at me.

2. To figure out what's up with the ghost in Uncle Gregor's basement. (If there really is a ghost in Uncle Gregor's basement. If not, I needed to get some help figuring out what's up with me.)

Then I wrote down what I could to do to try to make them happen.

1. Talk to Eli and tell him what's going on.

2. Do some research on ghosts.

3. Talk to the ghost and find out what she wants.

Mr. Z. had a poker tournament that afternoon, so I didn't need to visit him. That gave me some extra time. All I had to do was call Dad to check in, and take care of the goats once I got home.

It wasn't my best plan. But it was better than just waiting for Eli to stop being mad at me.

Eli's been my friend since the science center field trip in third grade. He loves tap dancing, hockey, and science.

I'm not really into hockey or tap dance, but I like science too. And I like hanging out with Eli.

Well . . . usually.

Today, Eli didn't say one word to me when I came into our classroom. I could tell he was still mad.

Back when we were little, when we first met, Eli tried to talk me into taking tap with him. "We could do it together. It would be fun."

"Nah, I'm more of a maker," I told him.

Eli didn't get mad that I said no, or decide it meant I didn't want to hang out with him. He just nodded. And ever since then, when Eli introduces me to someone, he tells them that I'm a maker.

That's how I know he's a good listener. And that's why I thought that maybe he'd still listen to me, even though he's mad at me, and why I wanted his help with this.

But he didn't wait for me at lunch. Maybe he didn't hear me when I called his name. Maybe.

So I took my lunch to the computer lab, and I typed up some questions for my experiment. I printed two copies, in case Eli ever decided to talk to me again.

After school, I got to the bike rack before he did, and I stood in front of his bike. "Eli, I know you're mad at me, but I need your help with something."

Eli crossed his arms. "I have to go to tap class."

"I know. But after your class, would you come help me record data for an experiment?"

"What kind of experiment?" he asked, still mad.

"I think there's a ghost in Uncle Gregor's basement. You know, because of yesterday," I told him. "But I need some help to see if it's just me or not."

Eli doesn't ignore stuff or pretend you didn't say it. He swung his bike helmet slowly back and forth by the straps. "Last Halloween you said you didn't believe in ghosts."

I nodded. "Right."

"And you know I don't believe in ghosts."

"Yeah, I know. But I want to revisit my position on this, and I need someone to be the skeptic."

"And this is a proper experiment, not you trying to scare me?" Eli asked.

I got a little mad then, although I tried to keep it

down. Grandpop says even when you have a right to be mad, you have to decide if you want to lead with that, because it doesn't always help people listen to you better. "I'm not a mean person, Eli. I don't scare my friends for no reason."

"I don't have good judgment on that," Eli said.

I sighed. This was because up until third grade, Eli thought he was friends with a kid, but then that kid turned out to be the kind of person who tells all your secrets to the whole school and then laughs at you. "Have I ever told your secrets to anyone? Come on, Eli. I need your judgment for this experiment."

Eli smiled suddenly. "Yeah, this is an area where *you* don't have good judgment! Okay. But no screaming for no reason. And I have to be home when my mom gets off work."

"Deal," I said. "We go, we write down our answers, and we discuss things calmly, like scientists. No matter what happens."

Eli nodded. "See you there at four."

"Thanks," I told him. "And if I'm right about the ghost, you owe me an apology."

Eli nodded. "I hope there's a ghost."

So do I, I thought. *I think.*

I needed to do some research, so I rode my bike to the library. I didn't have much time, so I didn't walk through the makerspace, where people can make Lego robots, crystal radios, and a whole lot of stuff out of duct tape. Nope, I went straight to the reference desk.

Harry was there today, wearing his bow tie that looks like an old-school library card. I like Harry. Before he came to work there, I kind of thought you had to be a white lady to be a librarian. I guess because all our other librarians were white ladies. But Harry's a Black guy, like me, and he likes learning all kinds of stuff too. (All the librarians do. It's their thing.)

"Hey, HD," Harry said, giving me the nod. "I hear the new *Spider-Man* comic will be here any day now."

I gave him the nod back. Talking to Harry feels comfortable, like when we go visit Mom's family in Oakland, where everybody knows what it means when you meet their eyes and nod your head, real slow. You're saying: I see you there. I respect you. Nobody looks at you weird there if you wear a cool hat, or asks you how your hair got like that, or if your dad is really your dad. People here don't always know that stuff, so I have to explain a lot. But when we go down there, it's Dad who sticks out, not me and Mom and Asad.

"Let me know how it is," I told Harry. "I need to read up on ghosts first."

"Like, *Ghostbusters*? Or Ghost Rider?" Harry asked.

"Not exactly," I told him. "They don't have to be comics. I'm looking for stories about how people wander around after they die trying to get stuff done, and what people can do to help them out. You know, ghost stories."

Harry smiled. "Do I have some ghost stories for you."

I told Harry I didn't need the ones where it was just someone fooling people, or anything about were-wolves or vampires or whatever. But he still found me a pretty good stack.

"Thanks," I told him.

"If you need more, you can always come back and ask," Harry said. "Though I hope you'll keep reading some comics too, or who am I going to talk to about what Ms. Marvel and Miles are up to now?"

"Yeah, you got it," I said. "As soon as I'm done with this project."

Harry nodded. "See you around, then."

"See you," I told him.

I pedaled fast, and made it to Uncle Gregor's house before four. I unlocked the door and opened it, very carefully. "Hello?" I said.

Nobody answered. I set my backpack down right inside the door, ran into the kitchen, and picked up the phone.

"Schenk Brothers Auto Body, do you need a tow truck?" It was Gloria, one of the other mechanics, not Dad. There was some kind of tantrum going on in the background.

"Nope, it's HD, calling to check in," I said.

"Well, your dad's trying to explain to a customer why he doesn't know how much it's going to cost until we know what's wrong with their car, Asad's having a meltdown about not getting any ice cream, and I've got someone on the other line," Gloria said. "You want him to call you back?"

"Nah, just tell him I called, I'm fine, and Eli and I are going to be at Uncle Gregor's for a while. I'll be home before he is. Thanks, Gloria."

"Okay, got it," Gloria said. "Have a good one."

I hung up the phone and hurried back outside.

It didn't take too long before I saw Eli riding down the street.

Eli parked his bike in Uncle Gregor's driveway. "So, what do you need me to do?"

I handed him a form and a pencil. "Come down to the basement with me, and fill this out."

Eli read the form carefully. "Okay."

I opened the basement door and looked around, but I couldn't see any thick air. Maybe the ghost hadn't heard us come in? I cleared my throat, and said, "*Hallo*, Great-Great-Grandma. *Wie geht es Ihnen?* It's HD, come to visit again. This is my friend Eli." My voice shook a little.

She floated her thick air out of the crock, but she didn't rush at me this time. She stayed near it, down at the bottom of the basement stairs. "*Guten Tag*, Hans Dieter. How nice of you to come to see me again. Do you make sauerkraut?"

"Nice to see you too," I said. Being polite is important, no matter who you're talking to. That's, like, a key rule of superhero stuff. It's weird to talk to someone you can see through, and not to be able to see their face or anything. But I know not to assume someone is the bad guy just because they turn green and enormous and their shirt gets too small to wear. I mean, so what if someone doesn't look exactly like you? Maybe whatever makes them look weird will help them save the world.

"I've never made sauerkraut, but I make other things," I told her. I started to relax a little, now that we were talking about making stuff, with no screaming or running or anything.

Eli had his pencil out, taking slow, careful notes. Eli always takes observations seriously.

"Uh, Great-Great-Grandma, we're here to do some research," I said. You aren't supposed to do research on people without them knowing about it. It's an important rule of modern science.

The ghost pretty much ignored me, though. "I was

famous for my sauerkraut," she said, nodding the thick air where her head would be.

"I bet it was great," I said. "Was this your crock? Is that why you're still here?"

"Yes, this is my crock," she said. She floated in a slow, sad little circle around her crock.

She didn't seem that happy to be there. And if I was dead, I knew I wouldn't want to hang around a pickling crock in Uncle Gregor's basement forever. I would want someone to sort stuff out so I could get moving. But what was my great-great-grandma waiting for?

"So, um, I want to figure out if my friend Eli can see you or hear you or not," I told her. "He thought I was playing a trick on him yesterday. I would really appreciate it if you would show yourself to him."

"Does he make sauerkraut?" the ghost asked.

"I don't think so," I said. "Hey, Eli, do you make sauerkraut?"

"What's sauerkraut?" Eli asked.

That sure set the ghost off. She went on and on about how great it was, and how to make it.

"You know, that stuff my dad puts on his hot dogs," I whispered to Eli.

"Why would a ghost care what your dad puts on his hot dogs?" Eli asked.

I shrugged, and started working on my own research form.

"I do not think your friend can hear me," the ghost said after a while, in a quieter voice. "Even my dear Hans Gerhard could not hear me. Once in a while, though, he would tell his mother he could smell my violet soap."

Violet soap. Well, at least that was something. "Did anyone else ever smell you?" I asked.

"No, no one at all." She sounded pretty sad. "Perhaps I should have faded away then."

I took a big sniff. I thought I might smell something—something kind of sweet. I made a note on my form. "I'm not sure if I can smell you or not, but I can definitely hear you."

"But why would I leave Hans Gerhard?" she went on. "So I practiced speaking. Every time he came into the attic, I would tell him all the steps for making sauerkraut. But he never heard me."

"Are you sure he couldn't hear you?" I asked. "I mean, maybe he just didn't feel like talking about your project right then."

She whooshed around the room, making the string hanging from the lightbulb swish. "If I told you all the steps for making sauerkraut, over and over again, all through your visit, and if, as you left, I told you how

41

much I loved you, how much I missed you, would you pretend I did not exist?"

Well, I could see how a situation like that might have been awkward for Hans Gerhard, no question there. But still. "No, I don't think so. That would have been really rude."

She stayed in one place, and her thick air looked a little thicker. Maybe she felt a little better, then? "Yes," she said. "Hans Gerhard was not a rude boy. So he could not hear me, no matter how much I practiced. And, after a while, he stopped visiting."

Maybe Eli wouldn't ever be able to hear her, then. I sighed. "Don't worry, Great-Great-Grandma. We'll figure this out."

"Done," Eli said, and handed me his research sheet.

I wrote out the rest of my answers, and handed it to him.

Even the ghost was quiet while we read.

- -

EXPERIMENT: CHECK TO SEE IF GREGOR
SCHENK'S BASEMENT IS HAUNTED

Researcher: HD Schenk

Do you hear anything? Yes

If so, what? *My great-great-grandma's ghost asking me when we're going to make sauerkraut, and telling me how great it is*

Do you see anything? *Yes*

If so, what? *My great-great-grandma (who looks like thick, moving air) swooping and swishing around the basement*

Do you smell anything? *Yes*

If so, what? *Something sweet. It could be her violet soap, because she told me that her grandson used to smell that sometimes. But I don't really know what violet soap smells like.*

Does the basement feel hot/cold/normal? *Normal, for a basement. It's usually cold down here.*

Conclusion: *Yes, the basement is haunted.*

- -

EXPERIMENT: CHECK TO SEE IF GREGOR SCHENK'S BASEMENT IS HAUNTED

Researcher: *Eli Callahan*

Do you hear anything? *Yes*

If so, what? *My friend HD arguing about something sour with nobody*

Do you see anything? *Yes*

If so, what? *My friend HD and a whole lot of boxes and some other junk*

Do you smell anything? *Yes*

If so, what? *Maybe mildew? Or maybe something sweet and mildew?*

Does the basement feel hot/cold/normal? *Cold*

Conclusion: *No, the basement is not haunted. It might be mildewy, though.*

After I finished reading Eli's research, my stomach felt funny, so I sat down on the bottom step.

"What is wrong?" the ghost asked.

I sighed. "Nothing is exactly wrong, Great-Great-Grandma—it's just that my friend Eli can't see you, or hear you."

"Right," Eli said. "Okay, what's the rest of the experiment?"

I blinked. "What do you mean?"

Eli turned his sheet over and examined the blank side. "Your hypothesis is that this basement is haunted, right?"

I nodded.

"But all we've done is record a few observations. We need to test things out."

"Uh . . . ," I said.

"Mrs.— Is it Schenk, or Davis, or something else?" Eli asked.

Great-Great-Grandma floated around until she was in front of Eli. She looked at him curiously. "I am Mrs. Marietta Schenk, young man." She hesitated. "Hans Dieter—you can call me Oma, if you like. It means 'grandmother.'"

I nodded. "Did you hear her that time?" I asked Eli.

"No," he said.

I sighed. "Mrs. Marietta Schenk," I told him.

"Is it okay if I call you Mrs. S.?" Eli asked. "Because I already call HD's mom Mrs. Schenk, and that could get confusing."

The ghost nodded, so I told Eli that would be fine. "I'm going to call her Oma, though, since she's my great-great-grandma."

"Okay, Mrs. S.: Could you please yell as loud as you can? This is for research."

Oma did her best. She wasn't that loud, but her

voice had a sad, cold sound that made the back of my neck shiver.

Eli watched me, and when I relaxed, he made a note. "One more time, please, Mrs. S.?"

This time I covered my ears.

"I guess that's enough, Mrs. S.," Eli said after a while.

I took my hands off my ears, and crossed my arms over my stomach.

"Do you want the garbage can in case you're going to puke?" Eli asked me.

I shook my head.

"Okay. Let me know if you change your mind." Eli finished his note. "Mrs. S., is there anything you can do to try to make me see you?"

Oma tried, she really did. She got bigger and wispier, smaller and denser, and she waved her air around wildly. She even did a loop-de-loop.

"She's over by the chain saw," I told Eli, who was staring at the hockey stick.

"Oh," he said, and stared at the chain saw for a while. "Okay, thanks, Mrs. S. Now, time for smells. Uh, Mrs. S., I would never ask you this if it was not for research, but could you please fart?"

I'm not sure which of us was more horrified: the ghost, or me.

"Certainly not," she said.

"Uh, Eli, I don't think she eats, so how could she do that?" I asked. "Besides, she says no."

Eli thought for a moment. "I think there was a ghost in a John Bellairs book that smelled like moldy graves once. . . . Can you do that?"

"Eli, she's not that kind of ghost. She smells like violets," I told him. "Oma, can we sniff you? For research?"

She wafted over a little, and I took a few steps forward.

Eli did too.

"I smell something kind of sweet," I said.

Eli sniffed hard.

"Can you smell it?" I asked.

He sniffed harder. "I don't know."

"Well, can you smell anything you didn't smell before?"

"Maybe," he said, still sniffing. "But maybe I just want to smell it." He made a note.

"Oma, can you go up to the top of the stairs?" I asked.

Up she floated, and that sweet smell went with her.

I sniffed again. Now I only smelled basement air, with a little bit of sharp-lemony old furniture. "I guess that was it."

Eli sniffed too. He nodded, and made a note. "Mrs. S., are you the kind of ghost that can walk through people?"

"She doesn't exactly walk," I said. "Also, what if she messes up your insides? Like, freezes them or something?"

Eli looked interested. "Mrs. S., can you freeze things?"

"I do not freeze things, and I do not pass through people," she said.

"Could you maybe try, though, for research?" I asked. "Uh, maybe let's see if you can freeze things first, and then you can go through Eli?"

Oma sighed.

"Wait here for a second," I said. I went up to Uncle Gregor's kitchen, got a glass of water, and brought it down to the basement. "Okay, can you freeze this?"

The ghost floated over to the glass of water and stuck a little of her thick air into it for a minute, kind of like she was sticking her finger in the water.

I thought the water moved a little, but maybe it was just still moving from when I put it down.

"I cannot," she said at last.

I walked over and felt the water. "Nope," I said.

Eli came and felt it too. We made notes.

48

"Maybe we should stop there," I said.

"No, this is for science. We need to do all the tests we can think of," Eli said. "Mrs. S., will you please float through me?"

"If you insist," she said, and started floating slowly toward him.

"She's coming your way, Eli. Are you ready?" I asked.

He bit his lip, clenched his fists, and nodded.

I held my breath as the ghost floated right through him. Eli didn't flinch.

"She's through," I said.

"Make a note that I do not like to do that," Oma said.

"Why not?" I asked.

"It is not the kind of thing a person does."

I made the note, and explained it to Eli.

"Well, of course a person doesn't do that—that's a ghost thing," he said. "But don't worry, it doesn't hurt."

"Did you feel anything?" I asked.

"Nope," he said.

Which should have made me feel better, because it would be awful if she'd accidentally frozen his insides. But I still didn't feel good. "I guess you really can't sense her," I said, looking at my shoes. "Or, maybe my

49

head isn't working right, and she isn't actually here at all. Maybe I need help. Maybe we should tell my parents."

"I thought I smelled something, though," Eli said.

I nodded. "But that isn't much proof, is it?"

"Hans Dieter, you are not crazy," the ghost told me. "I am right here."

"Thanks, Oma," I told her. "But I bet my brain would make you say that even if you weren't actually real." I bit my lip.

"You've been a ghost for a long time," Eli said. "Is there anything you can think of that will prove you exist?"

Oma floated there for a minute. "Perhaps one thing," she said at last. "But it might scare you."

"Is it dangerous?" I asked her.

"No, not dangerous. Just . . . surprising."

"She says there's something she can try, but it might surprise you, maybe even scare you," I told Eli. "She says it's not dangerous, though. What do you think?"

Eli looked nervous. But he lifted his chin up, and said, "Let's do it."

The ghost came right up in front of me, so close the whole room looked blurry through her thick air, so close that all I could smell was that sweetness. "Hans Dieter, I'm going to lift you up into the air. Are you ready?"

I lifted my chin up too. "Ready," I told her, and held my breath.

6

The ghost reached her blurry arms around me. I could feel something soft, something not-quite-there around my chest. I felt her tug me upward—

And then she stopped, and grunted. "You are a big boy, Hans Dieter."

"Well, yeah, I'm twelve, not some little kid," I told her. But I was positive I'd felt that. "Okay, try moving my hair instead."

I stood very still, and ghostly hands wiggled my locs.

Eli's eyes were huge. "Whoa."

"Did you see that?" I asked Eli, grinning. "Great work, Oma!"

Eli scribbled frantically. "Your hair moved, all right! We've got to test this."

After we confirmed that yes, my great-great-grandma could hear him just fine, even if he couldn't hear her, Eli designed another experiment.

EXPERIMENT: CHECK TO SEE IF
MRS. S. IS REAL

Researcher: Eli Callahan

Test #1: Ask Mrs. S. to lift the glass of water up in the air while HD stands at the bottom of the stairs.

Do you see anything? Yes, it fell over and spilled!

Test #2: Ask Mrs. S. to lift the glass up in the air while HD stands at the top of the basement stairs.

Do you see anything? Yes, some paper towels floated off of the workbench and cleaned up the water! Then they floated into the trash!

Test #3: Ask HD to go in the kitchen in case he's doing it somehow, without his knowledge. Then ask Mrs. S. to lift the hockey stick.

Do you see anything? *Yes, the hockey stick wiggled a little and fell over!*

Test #4 : *Ask Mrs. S. to lift HD's backpack while HD still waits in the kitchen.*

Do you see anything? *Yes! My pencil wrote: "Hans Dieter's backpack looks heavy, and I am tired" on my experiment sheet!*

- -

When I came back downstairs, Eli stopped making notes and looked at me. "I'm sorry I didn't believe you yesterday. And I'm sorry I got mad and didn't let you explain. That wasn't a very scientific thing to do."

"Apology accepted," I told him, smiling. "Thanks for helping me today."

"No problem," Eli said. "So, now what do we do?"

"We make the sauerkraut," the ghost told us.

I sighed. "Oma wants to teach me how to make sauerkraut."

"How do you make sauerkraut?" Eli asked the hockey stick.

"I will tell you how!" The ghost grabbed the pencil out of his hand and started writing down instructions.

Eli was carefully reading what the ghost was writing, sounding it out under his breath, so I was quiet and let him concentrate.

How to Make Sauerkraut

You will need five clean cabbages, some juniper berries, and a big box of pickling salt. You will also need a kraut cutter, a pickling crock, and a kraut pounder.

1. Set aside the outer leaves of the cabbages.
2. Slice the cabbages with the kraut cutter.
3. Mix some of the sliced cabbage with some of the juniper berries and some of the salt inside the pickling crock.
4. Pound the cabbage until it releases its juices.
5. Add and mix more sliced cabbage, juniper berries, and salt.
6. Pound again.
7. Continue until the crock is almost full.
8. Put cabbage leaves on top of the sliced cabbage in a thick layer.
9. Put the lid on the crock.
10. Fill the rim of the crock with water.
11. Wait 2-3 weeks, or until the sauerkraut is done.

I went over to the crock and examined it. It was bigger than my backpack. "That's going to be a lot of sauerkraut," I said.

"Yes, yes," Oma said, putting the pencil down and nodding the top part of her thick air. She seemed much happier now.

"What's a kraut cutter?" Eli asked.

Oma floated over and starting trying to yank something out of a box as though she'd been waiting fifty years for someone to ask that. (I guess maybe she had.)

"How do we know when it's done?" I asked.

"By the taste. When it is the best sauerkraut you have ever eaten, it is done."

"But I don't know what sauerkraut tastes like," I said.

"Then we will taste it together." She pulled harder at the cutter.

I explained all this to Eli. "I don't know if she can actually taste anything, though," I whispered, trying not to be rude.

Eli immediately turned to where the kraut cutter was moving. "Mrs. S., seeing as how you're a ghost, can you taste the sauerkraut?"

Oma's thick air froze in place. Very slowly she looked down at the kraut cutter.

"I think she's going to have to think about that," I whispered to Eli.

"That's fine," Eli said. "I have to get home anyhow."

"Me too," I said. "Oma, we have to go, but we'll be back tomorrow, okay?"

The ghost nodded. "Tomorrow, we can begin the sauerkraut!" she said.

I meant to tell my parents about Oma that night.

But first I had to take care of the goats. Then Mom wanted to know if Eli and I were still fighting, and after I told her we were done with that, she told me to go get my room ready for inspection. I cleaned things up and blew up the air mattress and got my sleeping bag and spare pillow all set up for Eli, and I passed Dad's inspection just fine. But then Asad had another tantrum about ice cream, all through dinner. Honestly, it was kind of a miracle we picked Eli and his mom up on time.

When we got home from waving goodbye to Eli's mom at the airport, it was pretty late, and my parents decided it was time for Eli to get settled, and for us all to get some rest (especially Asad). So I decided to wait to mention the ghost until I'd done more research.

Eli and I had a look through the books I'd gotten from the library.

"Maybe she's looking for one of her body parts," Eli said. "The guy in this one wants his toe back." He passed the book over to me.

"She's been dead for years," I told him. "Body parts don't last that long."

"Bones do," Eli said. "Maybe her toe turned into a fossil."

I skimmed the story. "Yeah, but look, all this ghost talks about is his toe, and all Oma talks about is sauerkraut."

"Maybe somebody stole her sauerkraut!" Eli said.

"Food doesn't last that long either," I said, giving him back the book.

"Fair point," Eli said. "What about yours?"

"Well, this one has a turnip field, but the guy that comes out of it doesn't want to cook the turnips or anything. And I'm not even sure he's a ghost. He could be a zombie." I sighed. "I'm not sure this writer did enough research."

"Maybe we need different books," Eli said.

"Or a different writer." I told Eli about Ms. Stevermer, the writer I met. "She said that sometimes ghosts stay until their Grand Purpose is completed."

Eli was looking through his book again. "Like if her body isn't buried in the cemetery where she wanted it?"

"How would I know where she's buried?" I asked.

"Well, we might need to improvise," Eli said. "Maybe we could ask that writer."

I shrugged. "We have to take the goats to see Mr. Z. tomorrow anyway. Maybe she'll be there again."

"We should take the ghost to visit Mr. Z. too. We can ask him if he knows what sauerkraut tastes like," Eli said.

I thought about it. "Uncle Gregor's house is kind of on the way. . . . We can ask Oma if she wants to come along, I guess. Then, if the writer is there, she can meet Oma too."

"Right! And after that, we can start setting up the Greatest Of All Time Obstacle Course!" Eli said. "Get it? It's the GOAT Obstacle Course—for goats!"

I grinned. Setting up an obstacle course in Uncle Gregor's backyard and training the goats to go through it was the very first thing on our list of fun things to do this summer.

I was really glad Eli and I were friends again.

The next morning, the goats were feeling playful, so it took a while to get them ready (although at least nobody pooped in the salt this time). They were pretty excited when we unclipped their leashes and let them run around Uncle Gregor's backyard too.

Eli followed me down into the basement.

"*Hallo*, Oma," I said. "Eli and I were wondering if you wanted to come with us to visit my friend Mr. Z. He has a friend who collects stories about ghosts."

"And he might be able to help us taste the sauerkraut too," Eli said. "We're going to ask him if he's had it before."

Oma floated up out of her crock and over to us. "Today, we will begin the sauerkraut!"

"Also, we were wondering something," Eli went on. "We don't know where your body is, or if it's where you want it, but maybe we could bury your crock?"

It's pretty hard to tell if thick air is giving your friend a look or not. But I thought she was.

"Maybe that would help," Eli said.

"Sometimes I put the sauerkraut in my root cellar over the summer, to keep it cool," Oma said.

"Um, right," I said. The trouble with trying to be

polite was that I wasn't too sure what kinds of stuff you weren't supposed to talk about with ghosts. "But don't you want to, you know, move on?"

"Move? Move where?" The ghost sounded surprised.

"Not move, exactly—move on. We thought maybe we could bury your crock in the cemetery and give you some peace or something," I explained.

She got very stern. "Young man, you cannot bury sauerkraut in a cemetery."

"No, ma'am," I agreed at once. "But . . . I don't know how to make sauerkraut."

"Not yet," she agreed, and this time I was sure she was nodding. "But I will teach you."

I turned to Eli. "Nope, she just wants to make sauerkraut with us."

"Yes! We can begin immediately!" Oma said.

"Well, no, not quite yet," I said. "First we have to take Mr. Z.'s goats to visit him, and maybe get some more information from his friend. You can come with us, or stay here, your choice."

She drooped a little. "I cannot leave my crock."

"Why not?" I asked.

"I do not know," she said. "When I moved into my crock, my son put it into a box, and took it up to the attic, and left me there, even when I asked him not to.

Everything was dark, for a long time. I tried and tried to leave, but I could not."

I explained all this to Eli.

"How did you escape from the attic?" he asked.

"One day, the box moved, and I went with it. When the box stopped moving, I was in a different attic, but still I could not leave." She sighed. "Many years later, I moved again, to here."

"Sounds like she came here with the crock when Uncle Gregor brought all of Grandma Schenk's stuff back," I told Eli. "I'm sorry, Oma. That sounds lonely."

"Sometimes I would turn on the radio. . . ." She floated over to the old radio on Uncle Gregor's workbench. "I would sing along, and hear what was happening in the world. But, in time, the batteries wore out, and everything was silent again."

Well, that explained why Uncle Gregor said they didn't make radios like they used to.

"We could bring your crock with us, if you want to come," I told her. It would look weird, but she seemed ready for a change.

She got very still. "You must be very careful with the crock. If it breaks, we will not be able to make sauerkraut."

"What if we figure out some transportation, and you can decide if it looks safe or not?" I asked.

"Thank you, Hans Dieter!" She swooped at me and pecked me on the cheek again.

I didn't flinch too much this time. In fact, it was kind of nice.

So we built a safety harness for the crock from an old hammock, to keep it from bouncing out of the rusty wagon we found, and wedged in some old towels so it wouldn't tip over.

Oma decided it looked safe enough to travel in, so Eli and I carried the wagon up out of the basement. Then I went back for the crock while Eli tried to convince the goats to let him put their leashes back on.

I wedged the crock in the wagon with the towels, covered it up with the hammock, and tied it down all around with some string and a knot I learned from my mom, who learned it from one of her friends in the navy. (Mom says the army is still best, of course, but those sailors do know some good knots.)

Then we set off for Maple Falls, with me pulling the wagon, and Eli walking the goats, and both of us trying to keep the goats from hopping into the wagon.

I thought Oma was ready to see the world, but after a few swoops, she dove back into her crock and stayed quiet. But it was nice to get to talk to Eli about the obstacle course instead of hearing more about sauerkraut.

When we got to Maple Falls, Mr. Z. was sitting by himself in the front garden.

"*Hallo*, Mr. Z.," I said.

"*Hallo*, HD. *Hallo*, Eli," Mr. Z. said, folding his newspaper. "Thank you for bringing my boys to see me." He scratched Rodgers on the chin and patted Hammerstein's head. (Mr. Z. doesn't usually speak much German when Eli is there, since Eli doesn't know German.)

"Hi, Mr. Z.," said Eli. "We brought someone to meet you."

Mr. Z. looked at the crock in the wagon. "Have you been frog-catching?" He handed each of the goats a carrot stick.

"Uh, no," I said, watching the ghost rise slowly from the crock. "Mr. Z., this is my great-great-grandma, Mrs. Marietta Schenk." Her ghostly air didn't look as thick as it had, but maybe that was because of the sunlight. "Oma, this is my friend Mr. Ziedrich."

"She's a ghost, so I can't see her or hear her. But HD can," Eli said helpfully.

Mr. Z. looked at me, his smile fading. Then slowly he looked at the crock.

"I didn't believe in her at first either," Eli said. "I mean, I believed that HD thought he saw her, but there wasn't any evidence that she was really there. But it turns out she can write with a pencil. Here, I'll get it." Eli dug his notebook and pencil out from under the hammock in the wagon. "Sorry, Mrs. S.—

the point got a little broken. But it should still write."
He held it up.

Oma floated up out of the crock and over to Eli.
Her air-hand moved close to his. . . . But then she sank
back down into the crock, without the pencil.

"Oma, are you feeling okay?" I asked, bending over
the crock. I could barely see her air. "Are you going to
move on now or something?" It was strange. I mean,
I'd only just met her, and she'd been dead a long
time—she probably wanted to move on. So I don't
know why I felt like I had a big lump in my throat.

"Wait, Mrs. S.—we still have a lot of experiments
to do!" said Eli.

"Um, boys . . . ," Mr. Z. said.

"Hang on a minute, Mr. Z.," I said. Her air wasn't
getting any thinner, but it wasn't getting any thicker
either. And either she wasn't talking or I couldn't hear
what she was saying anymore. "Oma, what's happening?" I grabbed the pencil from Eli and dropped
it into her crock.

Her thick air shivered a little, but the pencil didn't
move.

Eli frowned. "Maybe we shouldn't have taken her
out for a ride."

"I don't think she's getting worse," I said, not taking my eyes off of the ghost. "But I think something's
wrong with her. We'd better take her back."

"Do you boys need help?" Mr. Z. asked.

"Well, we need your help making Mrs. S.'s sauer-kraut, since we have to wait until it tastes right, and Mrs. S. doesn't have taste buds in her current state," Eli explained. "Unless she levels up today and moves on."

Mr. Z. looked bewildered. "Sauerkraut?"

"Yeah, she really wants to make it," Eli said. "Here, you can see our notes." He handed his notebook to Mr. Z.

Mr. Z. reviewed the pages, looking hard at Oma's sauerkraut recipe. "I see," he said at last. He examined the crock, and our faces, and nodded. "Then we will go at once, in the Maple Falls van."

"What about Rodgers and Hammerstein?" Eli asked.

"They will ride in the van with us," Mr. Z. said.

"Uh, Mr. Z., that van has carpet," I said. "You can't just hose it out. Maybe we should walk back instead."

Mr. Z. raised an eyebrow. "HD, I pay these people a lot of money, and they told me when I moved here I could use the van. Now, your . . . relative . . . needs our help. We will take the van."

8

I don't think the bossy Maple Falls guy liked having us load the dirty old wagon and Oma's crock into their fancy van, let alone me and Eli and Rodgers and Hammerstein. But Mr. Z. just plain didn't care. He asked that guy if the van was there for the residents and their family and friends or not. When the guy said yeah, Mr. Z. told him that we were his friends, so he should be more polite to us and put down some newspaper for the goats. And off we went.

Mr. Z. introduced us to Eleanora, the van driver, and I gave her directions to Uncle Gregor's house. It turned out Eleanora had gotten her car fixed at Dad and Uncle Gregor's shop, and of course she knew my mom (everyone knows my mom), so once we were away from the bossy guy, we were good.

I kept a close eye on the ghost. I thought she moved her air a little, but I couldn't hear her at all. I wasn't an expert on ghosts yet, but this didn't seem like leveling up to me.

"Do you think we took her too far?" Eli asked.

"Maybe, or we kept her away too long. But it doesn't make sense—she moved to Uncle Gregor's house without any issues."

When we got there, I left Oma's crock and the wagon in the van for a minute while Eli and I put Rodgers and Hammerstein in the backyard and cleaned up the newspaper. Then Eleanora let us take the wagon down with the van's lift.

Mr. Z. gave Eleanora five bucks and suggested she go have a cup of coffee, his treat, and said he'd call her when we were done.

I got Oma's crock out of the wagon, led the way into the basement, and set the crock on the workbench.

Almost immediately Oma flowed up out of it. "Where is my lid?" she said, and began rushing around the basement.

"Whoa!" I said, and ducked.

Mr. Z. looked at me, worried.

Which reminded me that we hadn't finished our

introductions. "Oma, could you come say hello to Mr. Z.?"

Oma zoomed over, snatched the pencil out of her crock, grabbed Eli's notebook, and wrote *Hello*. She floated it in front of Mr. Z.'s face. Then she dropped the notebook and zoomed off again, forgetting to give the pencil back first.

Mr. Z. put his hand on the basement stair railing. I saw it was shaking a little. But Mr. Z.'s hands do that sometimes. Dad says it's part of getting old.

"Does that mean she's feeling better?" Eli asked, picking up his notebook.

"Yeah, I think so," I said. "She wants to know where her crock lid is, so I'd better help her look."

Eli found another pencil on the workbench. "Mr. Z., we should do some research while you're here. Do you hear anything?"

Mr. Z. stared at the crock some more without answering. Then he took Eli's pencil and notebook and sketched something. He held it up. "The lid might look like this, with a knob at the top."

"Hey, Mrs. S., does your lid look like this?" Eli held up the notebook.

"Yes, like that, and brown," she said, nodding.

"She says yeah," I said. "Did you see it around here?"

"No. My grandmother had one very much like it," Mr. Z. said. He sounded kind of dazed.

"Do you smell anything, Mr. Z.?" Eli asked.

Mr. Z. sniffed. "Violet soap," he said wonderingly.

"And maybe some mildew too?" Eli asked. "We think that's just the basement, not the ghost."

"Yes, precisely," Mr. Z. said with a small smile. "Violet soap, and a little bit of basement mildew."

Eli made a note.

"Hey, Oma, can you sense the lid anywhere?" I asked. "You know, with your ghostly powers or whatever?"

The ghost stopped for a minute. "No," she said, and started zooming around again.

I watched the ghost rush wildly around all the boxes, wondering how long it was going to take to find the lid, and what kind of mess I'd have to clean up later.

Then again . . . "Oma, can you float through this stack of boxes and see if the lid is in any of them? Or is it too dark for you to see in there?"

"The rods and cones in your eyes can't work without light," Eli pointed out.

"Right, for our eyes—but she, uh, she doesn't have rods and cones anymore," I said. (She didn't have eyes anymore either, but I felt like it might hurt her feelings to point that out, especially in front of Mr. Z., since he still had his rods and cones.)

"Good point!" said Eli. "Let's test it out!"

Oma disappeared into the top of the first stack of boxes. The pencil she'd been holding fell to the ground. Then she oozed out the bottom with a little puff of dust that made Mr. Z. jump. "It is not there," she said unhappily.

"Keep looking, Oma. We'll find it," I told her.

Eli was asking Mr. Z. if he felt cold, hot, or regular when Oma made a noise like she was going to cry.

"Uh-oh," I said. I put the magazines I was holding back in the box and hurried over to her.

She was puffing in and out of the second box from the bottom of a stack. "Hans Dieter, my lid is broken!"

"Well, let's see if we can fix it." I moved the other boxes aside so I could open it. Sure enough, there were five pieces of brown pottery lid inside. "What glue should we use for this?" I asked Mr. Z., bringing the pieces over.

Mr. Z. fitted the pieces together carefully while Oma hovered nearby. Only a tiny piece was missing. "Silicone sealant, I think—be certain the package states that it is food safe! And, hmm." He looked out at the dim basement. "Er, Mrs. Schenk? Would you prefer that the lid be more useful, or more beautiful?"

Oma snatched Eli's pencil, making us all jump, and wrote *USEFUL*. Then she underlined it about five times in case we didn't get the picture.

Mr. Z. nodded. "If you fill in this gap with the silicone sealant, it will be airtight, and you can use it for the sauerkraut."

"Thanks," I said. "Okay, Oma—Eli and I need to go get the right kind of glue. We'll be back soon."

Thank you, Oma wrote.

"I will call Eleanora," Mr. Z. said, setting the pieces down on the workbench. "HD, I think that your parents would like to meet Mrs. Schenk."

I sighed, and nodded. Part of our deal is that Mr. Z. has to tell my parents if there's anything he thinks they might want to know about, if I don't. And I didn't mean to keep the ghost a secret anyway. I just wanted to work a few things out first. "Yeah, I'll introduce them tonight when they get home. Is it okay if we take the goats home and ride over to Rose's to get the glue?"

Mr. Z. nodded. "Yes, but take the bike path, check the intersections before you cross, and no stopping anywhere else along the way."

I guess not every town's hardware store has electronic supplies and a junkyard too. But Rose's RadioJunk-YardBirds has the perfect combination of stuff for a maker like me.

Eli went right to the glue section, but I needed to walk by the computer components first. I got as close as I could without breathing on the glass case, so I could double-check the specs on the CPU box I was considering. It was exactly what I needed—if I had a hundred dollars.

"Hey, HD. You want to see anything today?" Grace asked.

"Nah, not today," I said.

Grace nodded and went back to unpacking head-phones. Grace was the first Black geek I ever met, before Harry came to work at the library. She told me about how she learned to build computers in the army, and I told her maybe I'd learn to do that too, when I grew up. Grace just looked at me and asked what I was waiting for. She says it doesn't matter how old you are, or what you've learned—being a Black geek is about who you are, and what you're interested in. Nobody gets to decide that but you. So, I've been a Black geek ever since.

When Grace got out of the army, no one wanted to hire her to build their computers right then, so she used to work for my mom's farm program. But after Rose caught Dennis giving me a bad time when I asked to see some headphones, she fired him and hired Grace to manage the tech department. (I felt kind of bad for Dennis. I mean, he was a real jerk, and I used to peek in the window to see if he was there and not come in if he was working, so I'm glad I don't have to do that anymore. But I don't think he thought Rose would actually fire him for being mean to a kid.)

When I got to the glue section, Rose was helping Eli.

Eli handed me the silicone sealant. "It's safe for food, see!"

"Are you working on a new project?" Rose asked, ringing me up.

I shrugged. "I'm sorting through my grandma's stuff."

"Well, if there's anything you don't need, bring it to Mei. It's a rare day when she can't see the possibilities in something," Rose said.

When I was little, Rose and Mei merged the lumber store and the junkyard and became partners. Then RadioShack closed, so they started carrying electronic supplies too. Mei makes sculptures for the junkyard's Upcycled Art gallery, and sets car doors aside for a local musician who comes and bangs on them to figure out what sounds right for his next album. She gives tours for environmental field trips too, so kids can see that you shouldn't just throw things away when you're done with them.

"Thanks, I'll keep an eye out. Say hey to her for us," I said. Then we rode back to my house, to have some lunch and work out our plans without the ghost interrupting.

TO DO:

FIX LID

Glue pieces together

Fill hole

Try to make it look okay so Oma isn't too sad about it

MOVE CROCK (AND OMA) TO HD'S HOUSE

MAKE SAUERKRAUT

Get five cabbages, some juniper berries, and a big box of salt (ask Oma how many juniper berries, and how big a box)

Slice cabbages (talk to Oma about the food processor)

Follow Oma's recipe

Wait 2 weeks

Ask Mr. Z. to taste it

GET READY FOR ELI'S DANCE RECITAL

Practice routine

Build skyscraper costume

Choreograph solo

Practice solo

BUILD GOAT OBSTACLE COURSE

Build equipment

Train goats to go through it

Make the best video ever

SORT OUT BASEMENT

Open every single box

Sort everything out into stuff we can use, stuff someone else can use, and trash

Get paid

MAKE HD'S COMPUTER

Work on list of steps

Buy components

Put it all together

Oma was glad to see us again, I guess. She started right up about how we needed to make sauerkraut.

"Well, first we need to fix your lid, and then it needs to dry," I told her, reading the glue instructions.

"Mrs. S., can I talk to you about something?" Eli asked, and she floated over and grabbed the pencil out of his hand.

I got a damp rag from Uncle Gregor's kitchen and started wiping all the dust off of the crock and the lid pieces while Eli negotiated with Oma. He said it felt more equal when they were both writing. At least it meant they were quiet for a while.

"Gross," Eli said, coming over and examining my

dirty rag. "I bet Mrs. S. didn't like all that dust. Good thing she doesn't have allergies, or eyes, or a nose, or—you know."

"No kidding." I wiped it out again, and then one last time. "How'd it go?"

He handed me the piece of paper. "She's good with the food processor."

Eli: I know your recipe says to use the kraut cutter, but it looks like a super-sized version of this special slicer called a mandoline that my mom accidentally cut her finger really bad on. So I don't think HD's mom will let us use it.

Oma: As long as you are careful, you will not cut your fingers.

Eli: Right, and I am careful—I was extra-careful when HD let me light the last rocket we launched—and here, you can hardly see the scar at all now, right? But my mom says no way, no open flames and no sharp objects until I can keep better track of where my hands are at all times.

Oma: Hmm.

Eli: But since you've been dead, scientists have invented a machine that will cut cabbage

with the press of a button, in seconds! And
it has a special sensor so it won't let you cut
your fingers off. My mom says even I can
use it.

Oma: Where is this machine?

Eli: HD's mom has one—she got it before she
told Mr. Schenk he could never again buy her
a birthday present with a cord.

Oma: We will go there, and we will try this
machine, and we will make the sauerkraut.

Next, Eli showed Oma his dance moves, and sang
the music for her, and told her which parts were the
hardest, while I assembled my supplies: the glue, all
the lid pieces, and a bunch of paper towels.

I fitted the pieces of the lid back together, like Mr.
Z. had, so I could be sure where they all went before I
opened the glue.

"On the avenue I'm taking you to—FORTY-
SECOND STREET!" Eli belted out, shuffling his feet,
while Oma hummed along.

I opened up the silicone sealant and squeezed a
tiny bit onto a paper towel, to see how fast it came out,
and how much. Then I took a deep breath, picked up
the first piece, and squeezed it along the broken edge.

"Okay, this part is hard—" There was a thud, like maybe Eli ran into some boxes or something.

I didn't look up. Eli would tell me if there was a problem, and it's better to stick pieces together right after you put the glue on. Carefully I pressed the next piece onto the glued edge, turning it around so I could see if any extra glue dripped out. I held them together for another minute, then squeezed some glue along the next broken edge.

"Let's take it from the beginning," Eli said, and started over, with Oma singing along. "Hear the beat of dancing feet . . ."

I tried to tune them out while I concentrated. There was a bad moment where I didn't get two of the edges lined up quite right, but I caught it before the glue set, and wiggled them into place without any of the others falling off.

Finally, all the pieces were stuck together in their places. I squeezed a drop of silicone into the gap where the tiny piece was missing, and smeared it around with the glue nozzle to make sure it filled the little hole.

"BA-dum! DA-dum! Bu-BA-dum! Wop-wop— Fo-orty . . . SECOND STREET!" Eli yelled. I could hear his sneakers sliding across the basement floor in his grand-finale move, just as I put the glue cap back on.

"Bravo!" shouted Oma.

"Whoa!" Eli yelled. "HD, come here!"

I looked up.

Eli had backed up against a stack of boxes. He was staring right at Oma.

I stared too. "Oma, what happened? Why are you wearing your pajamas?"

Because she wasn't just thick air anymore—she was a glowing ghost. Still see-through, but now I could see the wrinkles on her face and hands, and the buttons on her pajamas.

Eli blinked. "I need to make some notes."

Oma looked down at her glowing pajamas. "Well . . .

if I had known that I was going to die then, I would have gotten dressed." She looked up again, staring back at me.

Wait—had she been able to see me clearly before? Or had I looked as blurry to her as she did to me?

Maybe she didn't know I didn't look like her grandson, or any of the other blond, blue-eyed Schenks she knew before.

I swallowed hard. I'd had a lot of practice explaining why I don't look like my dad. But not to my own great-great-grandmother.

She floated slowly toward me, still staring. It was creepier to be able to see a person flying through the air at you, even if she was see-through, and glowed and stuff.

I kind of froze up when she reached for me. Then I realized she was giving me a hug.

"Thank you," she whispered.

It didn't feel like a regular hug. But it was still nice, once I knew she wasn't going to pass through my body or anything.

"Everything okay?" Eli asked, his eyes big.

"Yeah," I said. "We're good."

EXPERIMENT: CHECK TO SEE IF MRS. S.
IS REAL, PART TWO

Researcher: Eli Callahan

Do you hear anything? Yes

If so, what? A ghost yelling "Bravo!" for my
tap dance! Then my friend HD asking a ghost why
she's wearing her pj's—and then I heard the ghost
answer!

Do you see anything? Yes

If so, what? Blurry air, moving around

Do you smell anything? Yes

If so, what? The same sweet smell, only
stronger (also mildew)

Does the basement feel hot/cold/normal?
Cold, but the same as last time

Conclusion: I think Mrs. S. really is floating
among us. (Don't get mad, HD, I believed you
before. But it's kind of different when you can
see someone with your own eyes.)

"When did you fix her lid?" Eli asked, still making notes.

"Right before I looked up and saw her like this," I told him.

Eli nodded. "So they could be related. Now that her lid is fixed, you can see her better, and I can hear her, and kind of see her." He made another note. "Hey, Mrs. S. Can you try lifting that hockey stick? I want to see if you've gained muscle mass—er, ghostly strength."

Oma floated over to the hockey stick and lifted it about a foot off the floor.

"Nice!" Eli said. "It's like you've been working out!" He bit his lip. "Uh, HD, maybe we could wait on having her yell? Or pass through me?"

"No problem." It was good to know that Eli wasn't quite so cool about this stuff after all—at least, not now that he could kind of see her.

"Hey, Oma, come check this out and see if it's okay," I called, holding up her crock lid.

She rushed over, the buttons on her pajamas glowing.

I wouldn't say it was my best maker work or anything. But it was food safe, like Mr. Z. said, and it was the best I could do.

She inspected the lid, and nodded. "Thank you, Hans Dieter," she said, giving me another hug.

"Any time," I told her when she let go again. "It needs to dry longer before we move it, though."

"We must find the kraut pounder so we can make the sauerkraut!" she said, taking off for another stack of boxes.

Carefully I wrapped masking tape around the lid so that all the pieces would stay in the same places even if they got bumped.

"Looking good!" Eli said, coming over to see it. "Now come here and check this out!"

I set the lid aside on the workbench, and sat down on the steps to watch Eli's routine and holler, "Yeah, man!" when he got the time step right.

After that, Eli worked out some ideas for his solo, and I started opening boxes.

The first one had an old plastic mixing bowl and some dish towels in it. "Hey, Oma, did you ever use this?" I asked.

She poked her head out through the side of a box and examined the bowl. "That is not mine," she said. "And this is no time for baking. We must make sauerkraut!"

"Got it," I said, putting the bowl in the pile of things to give to someone else.

"I have found it!" Oma cried, sticking her head through a different box. She floated out, and tried to lift the top box down. It fell to the floor with a crash.

Eli and I went over to help. Nothing broke, thank goodness—it was full of old screwdrivers and boxes of nails and stuff. We lifted the next box down, and took off the lid.

"The kraut pounder!" Oma cried, lifting up something that looked kind of like a wooden club with a flat bottom and top. "Now we are ready!"

10

I asked Oma to stay in the crock while we wheeled it to my house, but she said the motion made her tummy feel funny, and it was worse when she was inside the crock and couldn't see where she was going.

Eli pointed out that she didn't have a tummy. But neither one of us wanted to clean up ghost puke, even if no one in the history of science had ever examined it before.

"I am not going to vomit," the ghost said. "I am going to make my famous sauerkraut, and enter it into the fair, and win."

"Wait—what fair?" I asked.

Oma looked at me impatiently. "My sauerkraut must win the pickle prize at the county fair."

You know how someone proclaims something in comics, and it looks like the caps lock got stuck on? And you can tell you should remember what they said, because it will be important? Well, the ghost proclaimed that.

"I guess that's what she needs to level up and be at peace," I told Eli. At least it was easier than trying to find her fossil toe or something.

"It is very rude to talk about someone who is right here," Oma said, rushing around until she was floating in front of us.

"Sorry, Oma," I said. "We'll do our best to help, but it's up to the judges who gets a prize."

Oma frowned. "It is not just a prize. The winner is crowned the Pickle Queen. She wears the winner's corsage and her best hat, and she rides through the town in the mayor's car in the parade. It is a great honor, and everyone congratulates her throughout the year on her victory."

"Um," I said, and stopped. Eli and I looked at each other. Life back then must have been really different.

"I've never heard of the Pickle Queen," Eli said. "Maybe it changed since you died."

We turned down my street, the wagon wheels creaking over the bumps where the roots of the big old maple trees had lifted up the sidewalk.

"Here we are," I told the ghost as we rolled up our driveway, past Mom's vegetable garden. At least, no one else was home yet.

I carried the crock into the kitchen and set it down on the counter.

"Excellent. Let us begin," Oma said.

"Wait, we need to make sure your lid is dry first," I said.

Before I could stop her, Oma ripped the masking tape off of her lid and poked at it. "It will do," she announced.

I sighed. The instructions said to wait until the glue had fully cured, but I didn't see how I was going to convince Oma to wait forty-eight hours to use her lid.

"We don't have our supplies yet," Eli said.

"And I've got stuff to do too," I added.

"Like what?" Oma asked.

"Like moving a hay bale for Mr. Z.'s goats," I told her.

"Then we will make the sauerkraut after you feed the goats," she said, folding her ghostly arms.

Yeah, she was not going to settle down until we got her sauerkraut going. "Fine. I'll call Mom and ask her to get the cabbages and juniper berries and salt on her way home. But after I call her, you need to let me feed the goats, okay?"

"Very well." The ghost waited.

So I called Mom. "Hey, can you stop by the store on your way home? Eli and I want to try something."

"Hey, sweetie. What do you need?" Mom asked.

I checked the recipe. "Five cabbages, some juniper berries, and a big box of salt."

"What for?" she asked. "You're going to tell us all about this before you start making anything, right?"

"Sauerkraut," I told her. "It's . . . Well, I'll tell you all about it when you get home, okay?"

"That's a lot of sauerkraut," she said. "Especially since I don't think you've ever tried it."

I hesitated. "It's for someone else."

There was a pause. "Well, that's a lot of sauerkraut for Mr. Z. too," she said. "But I guess it will keep for a while, and your dad will like it. Tell you what: I'll pick up your cabbages, and we'll look at your recipe when I get home. If you don't need all five, I'll teach you how to make your grandmom's coleslaw. Deal?"

Maybe she'd have better luck convincing the ghost than I had. "Deal," I said. "Will you get the salt and the juniper berries?"

"Check in the pantry first and see what we have. I think there's a box of pickling salt on the bottom shelf—look behind the kosher salt. And check that gift basket Rainbow Carrot Farm gave me for my birthday—there were some unusual spices in there."

"Got it," I said. "Hang on a minute." I put the phone down and opened the pantry.

Oma floated over to see what I was doing. "Aha!" she cried, swooping down toward a blue box.

"Is there enough left in there?" I asked. "Or do you need a whole box?"

The ghost lifted the box carefully. "No, this will do." She set it down again.

I picked it up and put it on the counter. Then I dug around in Mom's gift basket until I found a little jar labeled JUNIPER BERRIES. "Oma, do these look right?"

She grabbed the jar and tried to open it, but she couldn't get a good grip. "We must smell them and see if they're too old," she told me, handing it back.

I opened the jar and held it out so she could sniff it.

"Yes!" Oma cried, and did a little circle in the air. "We are ready!"

"Almost," I told her, shutting the pantry. Then I picked up the phone again. "Yeah, we've already got some salt and some juniper berries, Mom. Thanks."

"Okay, good. Then I'll see you soon. Love you, sweetie."

"Love you too, Mom." I hung up. "Okay, Mom's getting the cabbages. So now I'll feed the goats. You coming, Eli?"

"Sure," Eli said. He loves using the hay-loader. "Do you think we should take the ghost with us?"

Oma glared at him.

I sighed. "Why don't you ask her what she wants to do? She's right here, and she's old enough to decide for herself, Eli."

"Sorry, Mrs. S.," Eli said. "Do you want to come out back and feed the goats with us?"

"No, I will stay here," she said. "You can get out that slicing machine you told me about and some vegetables, and I will try it."

"Okay," I said. At least, it would keep her busy.

"So, you have to wash the vegetables before you put them in the food processor," Eli told the ghost. "Can you turn the water on and off? Wait, did they have indoor plumbing when you were alive? What about electricity? Do you know how this all works?"

"I died in 1961, not the Dark Ages," Oma said stiffly. "I know how it works." Slowly she turned the cold water on to a trickle, and then off again.

"Good job," I told her. I got out the food processor and the grater blade and set it up for her. Then I got a few carrots out of the fridge and set them next to the sink. "Now, let me show you how this thing works."

The ghost watched as I washed a carrot, put it on the cutting board, cut off the top, cut the carrot into big chunks, put the chunks in the tube, stuck the pusher in, and pressed the button. "This is a very nice machine," she said.

I nodded. There really isn't much you can mess up with a food processor. She'd do fine.

"Bye, Mrs. S.!" Eli said. "C'mon, HD." He headed out the door.

"Bye, Oma," I said, and followed him.

Rodgers and Hammerstein were definitely glad to see us again. They jumped up on the hay-loader platform as soon as I lowered it, and then they had a contest with Eli to see who could jump the highest (Hammerstein won).

Then Eli and I got the next hay bale out of the garage and lifted it onto the hay-loader's platform.

The hay-loader was my first real invention. Hay bales are heavy, and goats eat lots of hay—and they won't eat dirty hay, so you can't just leave it on the ground; you have to put it in a manger for them. It's hard lifting a whole hay bale up into their manger by myself because the sides are pretty tall, so I needed a solution. I went to the library, and Harry and I looked all over the internet, figuring somewhere out there was a farmer with the same problem as me. But we couldn't find anything.

So Mr. Z. found me a design for a box lifter, and then I modified the design and built it and hung it from a big old apple tree in our backyard. Now I can strap a hay bale onto the platform, winch up the ropes, swivel it around until it's over the manger, and release it so it falls right in.

It took a lot of tries to get the design right. But the first time it really worked . . . Well, that was probably the best moment of my whole life. Mr. Z. said he'd never seen a better-designed solution, and Mom asked if she could share the design with some of the farms she works with. I told her sure.

It was my project for the science fair last year, but I couldn't build an operational one in the multipurpose room because they wouldn't let me hang it from the ceiling. The judges weren't goat farmers, and they didn't really understand my diagrams, or how it helped people. I didn't win anything.

But Mr. Z. told me about patents, where you file some papers and diagrams that tell everyone you invented your cool design, and then by the time they realize what a great idea it is, it belongs to you and no one else can make it for a while without your permission. Mr. Z. has some patents from when he was an engineer. I'm working on the diagrams for my hayloader, and when I'm ready, he's going to file it for me, in my name and everything.

While we worked, I told Eli about how I'd been

thinking about some kind of door trap for my room so Asad wouldn't be able to get in and touch my stuff. Then Eli wanted me to watch a new solo dance, until Rodgers butted Hammerstein off the hay-loader and Eli tripped over him. And then we brainstormed some more ideas for the GOAT Obstacle Course.

"We should start working on it tomorrow," Eli said.

I sighed. "I guess we'd better go talk about sauerkraut some more first, though."

"It's okay," Eli said. "We've got all summer. We have time to help your great-great-grandma out."

"Hey, Mrs. S.!" Eli said as we came back into the kitchen.

There was no response. I looked around uneasily. The food processor was full of grated carrots, and she'd washed the knife and put it in the dish drainer.

"Where are you, Mrs. S.?" Eli asked.

"I don't think she's here," I said.

"What if she's already passed on?" Eli asked. "I mean, she doesn't ever have to go to the bathroom, right? So where else could she be? Do we still make the sauerkraut?"

"I don't know," I said.

There was a noise from the family room. We both froze.

I crept to the doorway, with Eli right behind me.

Oma was staring at the photos on the mantel, crying. (At least, bluish-white streaks were running down her bluish-white face, and she looked really sad, so I think she was.)

"What's she doing?" Eli asked.

"I think she misses her family," I whispered. "She's having a Captain America moment—like, when he came out of cryogenic stasis and realized everyone he knew lived the whole rest of their lives without him while he was frozen, and now he's back—but they're all gone."

"Should we ask if she needs anything?" Eli asked.

"She might need a moment first," I said. "We can get ready to make her sauerkraut, though. Maybe that will help her go see her family again."

So I found a container, scooped all the grated carrots out of the food processor, and put them in the fridge. I washed the food processor and Oma's kraut pounder too.

"Do you think we should check on her now?" Eli asked.

I dried off the kraut pounder and thought. Maybe seeing her kraut pounder all clean would make her happier. "Okay," I told him.

She was still crying, I think. But she turned around this time when we came in.

"I'm sorry you're sad," Eli said.

"Thank you," she said, sniffing. She turned back to the photos.

I went over and stood next to her. "That's my granddad." I showed her the one where he had his truck all apart in pieces and was holding a wrench and laughing. "Uh, your grandson, I guess."

She looked at it for a long time.

"And that's my dad and Uncle Gregor." I showed her the one where Dad still had the leg he was born with, and they were dressed up for some teenage thing. "Mom says I have Dad's chin."

She examined me. "She is exactly right—your father's chin, and your mother's eyes."

I showed her the photos of Mom and Dad dressed up in their uniforms for army balls and hanging out with some of the soldiers from their battalion, and the one from when they got out. "And here's Grandmom and Grandpop Davis, with Mom and Aunt Nia when they were little—and here's the last time we visited them, when we all went to see Kwame Alexander talk at their library."

"You have a brother?" she asked, pointing to another one.

"Yeah, that's my little brother, Asad." It was a photo of us at the air show last summer. Mom and Dad had their arms around each other. I was watching some lady spin a propeller, and Asad was about to have a meltdown. We looked good, though. Like the family we are.

I imagined what it would feel like, if they were all gone, and shivered.

"HD washed your kraut pounder for you," Eli said.

The ghost blinked. "Yes . . . we must make the sauerkraut." She floated into the kitchen, grabbed a clean dish towel, and gave the kraut pounder another swipe. "But that machine will not work. We need sliced cabbage, not grated cabbage mush."

I held up the slicer blade. "What if we use this instead?"

The ghost examined it. "Perhaps. . . . If you have another carrot, I will try it."

So I got out another carrot for her, and showed her how to take out the grater blade and click the slicer blade into place.

Then we all heard the front door open. "Hey, sweetie, I'm home!" Mom said.

I swallowed. Right. So what exactly was I going to tell my mom about all this?

11

"Hey, Mrs. Schenk!" Eli said. "We're doing some research!"

"Didn't I tell you two no experiments in the kitchen unless they've been cleared by an adult first?" Mom asked, coming in and setting her groceries down. She didn't say anything about the ghost who floated over to peek into her bags.

"But we're under adult supervision!" Eli said happily.

Mom studied me with her mom-abilities, like she could read my mind. "What's wrong?"

How do you tell your mom that the ghost of your great-great-grandmother is moving in with you for a while? Probably those people who work with the Avengers have a plan for this kind of thing, but I didn't.

Mom was looking at the food processor. "Honey, what's going on here?"

"We are ready to make the sauerkraut!" Oma said.

Mom didn't blink. She folded her arms and stared at me, waiting. I had about one second more before there were consequences.

I thought about what Grandpop Davis says, about how people might remember what you told them later, even if they can't hear it right then. "Um, Mom? We need to help my great-great-grandma make sauerkraut, for the fair."

"She's an adult," Eli explained. "I mean, she's a ghost, but she's an adult ghost. You never said an adult ghost couldn't supervise us."

I met Mom's eyes, so she'd sense I was telling the truth. "I want you to meet my great-great-grandma on Dad's side, only I guess you can't see or hear her. I'm not sure what's happening here either. But she's lonely, and she needs help making her sauerkraut. I'm not crazy, but I don't know how to prove that to you." I took a deep breath so I wouldn't cry. Someone had to be reasonable here.

Eli had gone back to taking notes. "Mrs. Schenk, how old are you?"

Mom stepped forward to feel my forehead. "Why do you need to know that?" she asked, right as the ghost said, "I was born in 1891, young man. You do the math."

Mom frowned at me, not a mad-frown, but concerned. "What's going on with you, sweetie? This isn't like you."

"You told me family takes care of family." I was breathing deep, like she taught me, so I could get my words out. "And every person has to make their own choice to do what they decide is right, no matter what anyone else does. Well, I'm trying to do the right thing, and I'm trying to take care of family. Just because Oma is a ghost doesn't mean she's not family."

Oma smiled at me, but it was a pretty sad smile. She started floating out of the kitchen again. I wondered if I should go see what was wrong now, but I knew Mom wasn't done with me yet.

"We're doing research on who can sense the ghost, and what the common factor might be," Eli said. "HD can see her and hear her way better than I can, and I guess you can't hear her at all. Maybe it's an age thing? Mrs. Schenk—I mean HD's mom—can you smell anything?"

Mom looked like she wanted to discuss that some other time, but she knows Eli pretty well. She sniffed.

"Carrots, I think—and something sweet . . . maybe vanilla?"

"Violets," I told her. "She smells like violet soap. Hang on a sec, Mom." I walked over to the doorway and stuck my head through it. "She's in the family room, crying again," I told Eli.

Mom looked at me for a long time. My mom doesn't need a Lasso of Truth to tell if you're lying, she just knows. "What's wrong?"

"Everyone she knew is dead, only they're not ghosts." I shrugged. "It's okay, Mom. I know I can't fix that. But I can't ignore her or leave her by herself. She needs her family, and she hasn't got anyone else left."

"She doesn't usually cry," Eli said helpfully. "Usually she talks about sauerkraut."

Mom took a deep breath. She looked at me hard, with her mom-abilities still dialed up to the highest power I'd ever seen. She took another deep breath. "Is she telling you to do anything?"

"She wants us to help her make sauerkraut," I said. "But that's it."

"Are you seeing or hearing anything else that is not a part of your everyday existence up until now?"

"Good question, Mrs. Schenk!" Eli said happily. "Are you, HD?"

I shook my head. "I'm not crazy, Mom, really."

Mom frowned. "You know we don't joke about mental health. We remember that help is available when we need it. But first we have to tell someone we trust what's going on." She gave me a look. "And we are supposed to tell that someone right away."

"Yeah, I know," I said. "I'm sorry I didn't tell you sooner. It won't happen again. But, Mom, I don't have mental-health issues. I just need to help my great-great-grandma make sauerkraut."

"We can have her lift something, to prove she's here," Eli said. "She's pretty good at it."

"Can you see and hear her too?" Mom asked Eli.

"Not as well as HD, but yeah, I can," Eli told her. "You get used to it. You have to remember, she can hear you, so try not to hurt her feelings."

"Okay," Mom said. "You're responsible boys, usually. You know we don't joke about this stuff. And you seem to believe what you're telling me. So show me what's going on here."

Eli ran over to the doorway. "Hey, Mrs. S.? Can you come lift a pencil so HD's mom can see you and know you're real?"

The ghost turned, those white-blue streaks still on her face, and swooped into the kitchen toward us. She grabbed Eli's pencil and the notepad by the phone and wrote, *My grandson is dead. My family is gone. I am alone.*

I heard my mom gasp.

"Hey, I'm part of your family too!" I said. "And I'm not gone!"

"And I'm HD's friend, so I'm almost like family," Eli said. "My school picture's on the mantel and everything. So you're not really alone."

My mom was staring at Oma's words. She reached out and touched the pencil that Oma had dropped on the counter. She looked up at the family-room door for a long moment.

Then she put her hands on her hips. "And you are my family too," she declared. "HD, tell me where she is. I think she needs a hug. Is she okay with hugs?"

"She's right next to the phone," I said. "I think you're okay with hugs, aren't you, Oma?"

Mom didn't wait for the ghost to answer. She went over and put her arms around the air right next to where Oma was. The ghost gave a little sigh, then ducked under Mom's arms and came up inside the hug.

"I'm sorry this happened to you," Mom said.

"It's not that bad," I said.

"Not you," she snapped. "Your great-great-grandma." She gave the air another little pretend-squeeze. Then Mom stepped back and dropped her arms. "Okay. Now, this is my house, so there are going to be some rules we all follow. HD, you can help your great-great-grandma, as long as she doesn't ask you to do anything your dad or I would say no to. Eli, you can help HD if you want to, as long as it's nothing HD's dad or your mom or I would say no to. Mrs. Schenk, you and I will have a discussion about the house rules later, and if I hear that you are asking anyone to do anything that is against my house rules, I will personally see that you are banished from this plane of existence." She waited.

The ghost wrote, *I will not do anything to hurt your family, or your friends.*

"Good. We're going to work with this for now. But if either of you starts hearing or seeing anything unusual that isn't directly related to this particular ghost, you are going to come talk to me or HD's dad immediately." She stopped, and sighed. "I need to call your dad." Then she looked back at the air by the phone. "Chores before sauerkraut, and no experiments unless Mr. Ziedrich, HD's dad, or I have approved them first. Got it?"

Eli and I nodded.

I understand, the ghost wrote.

"Thank you," Mom said.

"Hey, Mrs. S., how old was your grandson when you died?" Eli asked.

The ghost sighed. "He was twelve."

"So's HD, and so am I!" Eli told her. He wrote *12* with a big star next to it.

I took the trash out, and Mom called Dad, and then her sister. She wanted me to say hello.

Aunt Nia's cool. She's not a maker herself, but she gets why it's important to me. She works with kids who need some help with their problems. Sometimes she sends me articles about kids who made amazing stuff, even though their schools don't have a lot of money. Sometimes I send her Ironheart comics, because they're her favorites.

"Hey, Aunt Nia. That robotics team was cool," I told her.

"I thought you might like that," she said. "Now, your mom says you're spending time with a ghost. You want to tell me what's going on?"

I told her how I met Oma in Uncle Gregor's basement, and once I fixed her lid, Eli could hear her too, and see her, kind of, and how she wasn't telling me to break any rules, or making me feel bad about myself, she just wanted help making her sauerkraut so she could win the fair.

Then Aunt Nia had me put Eli on for a while so

he could tell her the whole thing from his point of view.

We tried to put Oma on next, but Aunt Nia couldn't hear her at all.

When I got back on the phone, Aunt Nia told me it was fine to want to know about all my roots, not just Mom's side, and I didn't need to invent a ghost to talk about that.

"Yeah, I know," I said. "We already talked about all that when Mr. Z. wanted to teach me German. I'm good with being German American too, even though people can't guess that's part of me by looking at me. Believe me, I don't need to go around inventing ghosts. I have my own project to do this summer."

"I see," Aunt Nia said. "How's that coming along, anyway?"

"Well, I haven't had a lot of time for it yet, what with helping Oma out," I told her.

"Mm-hmm," Aunt Nia said thoughtfully. "HD, you're a smart kid, and you're a kind kid, and I know you don't have a problem with helping people out. So I want you to keep something in mind for me: Your goals are just as important as everybody else's. When somebody asks you to set your goals aside to help them with theirs, I want you to consider the situation carefully. Do they really need your help? Are their goals truly more important than yours? And do they understand they're asking you to set aside your goals for theirs?"

"Oma's been waiting a really long time for this," I said.

"I can see that," Aunt Nia said. "But remember: She's already had her chance to be twelve, and to live her whole life. All I'm saying is, take some time to think about what's right for you, as well as what's right for her. Got that?"

"Got it," I told her.

"Good. Now, I'll tell your mom who she can talk to about all this, and she might want you to talk to them too. But in my opinion, you're doing just fine. So I'm going to tell Kikora that she should be glad that her biggest problem is a ghost wanting to teach her son how to cook. Sound good?"

"Thanks, Aunt Nia," I said.

"I've got one more piece of advice for you," Aunt Nia said seriously. "If I were you, I wouldn't go telling everyone you know about all this. It sounds like you're having a special experience that not everyone can relate to. Don't let me hear about you seeing anything else that no one else can and not telling your parents. But you don't have to share what you can do with people outside your family, if you don't want to."

"Yeah, like not telling everyone you're Spider-Man—don't worry, I know," I said. "It's only for a few weeks anyway. Eli and I think she's going to level up after the fair."

"Call me anytime you want to check in," Aunt Nia told me. "Now, put your mom back on so we can finish our talk."

Mom seemed a little more relaxed after that, and I felt better too. Cleaning my room wasn't so bad. I bet even the Justice League and the Avengers and the Men in Black need an hour where nothing weird happens sometimes. I mean, aside from your friend going upstairs to use the bathroom and reporting that your great-great-grandma is humming along with your mom and Janelle Monáe and maybe doing some ghostly dancing.

But I knew that ghost and her sauerkraut weren't going to wait forever. "Mom, I'm done," I said, coming back up into the kitchen with Eli.

Mom put a pan of chilaquiles in the oven. "Good work," she told me. "Eli, have you called your mom today?"

Eli's face fell. "I forgot."

Mom sighed. "Well, it's three a.m. in Edinburgh right now, so I guess you'd better call her tomorrow instead." She wrote a big note so Eli wouldn't forget again.

ELI: CALL YOUR MOM BETWEEN 9 A.M. AND NOON.

She added Eli's mom's travel cell-phone number and stuck it to the fridge. "I'll be at work by then. Do you need a reminder call?" (Mom used to do battalion logistics when she was in the army, and now she helps farmers sort out what they need to run their farms. She's really good at keeping people organized and on task. Sometimes she says we're as much work as a full battalion. But I always remind her that without Asad, we'd actually only be as much work as a quarter of a battalion, max.)

"Nah, I'll help him remember," I told her. "Sorry we forgot today. We kind of had a lot going on."

Mom nodded. "So, has your brother met your ghost yet?"

I shook my head. "He might not be able to see her, though."

Mom frowned. She picked up the pencil and paper and went into the family room.

Conversation Between
My Mom and Oma

Mom: I would appreciate it if you would wait to say hello to my younger son, Asad, until I ask HD to introduce you.

Oma: When will I meet him? Is he as helpful as Hans Dieter? He can help us make the sauerkraut too.

Mom: Asad is only six.

Oma: Hans Dieter is a very helpful boy. So is Eli.

Mom: Please try not to scare Asad.

Oma: I had a son, you know, and a grandson. I do not go around scaring little boys.

Mom: Have you met any since—you know— have you met any recently?

Oma: No, not since—not for a long time.

Mom: I see. When Asad and his father arrive, please go stand near HD, and don't move anything until we do introductions.

Oma: Very well. Please, call me Marietta. May I have your name?

Mom: I'm Kikora. I thought HD said your name was Oma?

Oma: Oma means grandmother. It is what my grandson called me. I can see you are a

good and loving mother to your sons, Kikora.
Thank you for having me in your home.

Then Eli and I presented our project plan for making sauerkraut to Mom. Project plans are something Mr. Z. taught me about, and Mom and Dad review mine before I start new projects.

We showed her Oma's recipe and told her we had all our supplies since she'd already picked up the cabbages we needed.

I drew a picture of the kraut cutter, and Oma explained how all you had to do was slide the cabbage along that really sharp V-shaped blade and keep your fingers out of the way. But Mom said under no circumstances were Eli or I to use one, that was an absolute deal breaker, and she was not going to explain to Eli's mom how he'd lost all his fingers at her house making sauerkraut with a ghost.

So I reminded Oma we could use the food processor instead, and Mom agreed that was a good solution, as long as we cleaned up after ourselves, and Eli didn't use the knives either.

I explained that Oma would be leading the project, since it was her recipe and her ghostly goal. Eli would wash cabbages and help pound, and stay away from knives. (Oma interrupted to tell Mom that no, we wouldn't be pounding it into obliteration like Eli said, since we wanted the sauerkraut to be crunchy, not pulverized.) I would cut the cabbages into chunks for the food processor, after cutting a flat part so the cabbage wouldn't roll around, and I'd help pound too. And Oma would run the food processor. She promised not to stick any of her ghostly essence into the food processor while it was running, since we didn't know what ghost blood might do to the sauerkraut, if she managed to cut herself.

"What if it gets moldy?" Mom asked. "One of my farmers told me she tried making sauerkraut, but it got moldy, and she had to throw the whole batch out."

"My sauerkraut will not be moldy! At least, not if all the cabbage is properly covered." Oma hesitated. "Though, there is a stage where it smells—but only a little bit."

"She says it won't get moldy as long as we keep it covered," I told Mom, right as Eli said, "She says it might stink. Hey, Mrs. S., what does it smell like?"

Mom folded her arms. "If this kitchen starts to smell, we will revisit this project. And I reserve the right to throw out any sauerkraut that goes moldy, or stinks, or does not look safe to eat. Are we clear?"

"What kind of world is this, where people might

throw out good food because it smells a little bit?" Oma said.

But she said it pretty quietly, and she didn't write it down for Mom to answer. "Yeah, we're clear, Mom."

"Don't worry, Mrs. S. If it starts to smell, maybe HD can set up a fan or something. Or we could move you to the garage," Eli told her.

Then Mom and Oma had a one-page discussion about why it was so important to make an entire crock full of possibly smelly sauerkraut, and Oma assured her that yes, it would all get eaten, and how she would teach Mom and Dad a bunch of recipes that she couldn't believe they didn't already know, all using sauerkraut.

I guess that wore Mom out, because after that she agreed to let Oma keep her crock in a corner of the counter and live (or, you know, ghost, or whatever) in our kitchen. Project approved!

So I got out the kitchen scale and weighed all the cabbages and the salt, and measured all the juniper berries we had in teaspoons, and Eli made notes on the recipe about what we had when we started.

"Attention!" Eli said in his hockey announcer voice. "Folks, you are about to see Mrs. S. make her first sauerkraut in over fifty years—"

"These are good cabbages," Oma interrupted, inspecting them carefully. "Tell your mother she has chosen well."

"And . . . Mrs. S. compliments Mrs. Schenk on her choice of cabbages!" Eli cried.

Then Oma floated over and hovered next to him until he started washing them.

Once he'd handed the first one to me, Oma told me exactly which leaves I should pull off and set aside before I cut the cabbage. (They all looked the same to me, but it was her project, so I did it her way.)

"Mrs. S. puts the first cabbage chunk into the food processor . . . ," Eli announced. "She's pushing the button . . . and . . . SLICED! She asks HD for an assist: Can they take the machine apart and see how the cabbage looks? The crowd holds its breath as Mrs. S. inspects the cabbage . . . and—SHE SAYS IT WILL DO! The crowd goes wild!" (Here, Eli played the part of the crowd going wild, until Mom stuck her head in and said that was enough, and could he put some music on?)

The food processor filled up fast. "Should I dump it right in the crock?" I asked.

"Yes, put it into the crock," Oma said. "Now we sprinkle it with salt, and add the juniper, and mix it around."

So I sprinkled salt in until Oma said to stop. Oma added the juniper berries herself.

"Now, mix it around, yes, with your hands— CLEAN hands! Now then, yes, like that."

It felt like making a sandcastle out of crunchy seaweed. I let Eli pound it while I washed the salt off my hands.

When Oma told him to stop, the cabbage looked kind of wet, with little black juniper balls mixed in.

"Is it supposed to look like that?" I asked her.

"Yes, juice comes out of the cabbage and mixes with the salt, and that makes the brine," she said. "More cabbage, please!"

So I cut up the next cabbage. Since he'd finished washing all the cabbages, Eli made us all iced teas with lemonade, including the ghost, so she wouldn't feel left out. We sipped our drinks while Oma sliced the cabbage and sang along with Ella Fitzgerald, when we could hear the music over the food processor. It turned out Oma had listened to her back in her day too.

Eli made up a tap dance for "Mack the Knife," and we all clapped and cheered, until he crashed into the table and Mom stuck her head in again and suggested he take a break.

Every few minutes, the food processor would fill up, and Oma would hover over me and remind me what to do while I dumped the cabbage into the crock and added salt, even after I told her that thanks, I thought I'd got the hang of it. Then she'd add the juniper, and Eli and I would mix and pound it.

When I cut up the last cabbage, Eli started announcing again. "HD passes the last cabbage chunk to Mrs. S.! Mrs. S. drops the cabbage straight into the chute— she's pressing the button now—and GOAL! All the cabbage is sliced! Now it's back to HD. He dumps the cabbage into the crock—he sprinkles it with salt—Mrs. S. adds her special ingredient—HD mixes it up—and Eli picks up the kraut pounder and starts pounding it—yeah, carefully, I know. Mrs. S. tells HD to put the cabbage leaves on the very top and . . . the crowd waits to see what Mrs. S. thinks."

Oma was examining the crock. It was almost full of cabbage and salt. Mom was right: that was going to be a lot of sauerkraut.

"We will check it again tomorrow. If enough juice has not come out of the cabbage, we must add brine made with water," Oma said. "The cabbage must be covered in brine, or mold could form."

"Got it," I told her. I picked up the box of salt and weighed it again. I wrote down the current weight, then subtracted it from our starting weight, so I could write down how much salt we'd actually used. Then I measured out the juniper berries, and subtracted that from the original amount too. Oma might be a sauerkraut expert, but I thought the judges might want real measurements.

"Can I see?" Mom asked, coming in and peeking into the crock.

Oma smiled. She floated over and got the pencil and paper. *Do you make sauerkraut?*

Mom said, "No, but—"

Then I heard Dad's Fiat pull up into the driveway. "Um, Oma, do you think it's making enough brine?" I asked her, poking the cabbage leaves with the kraut pounder.

Mom slipped out of the kitchen.

I heard the front door open.

"Not yet," Oma told me. "It may take longer. Put the lid on now, and fill the channel with water, so the sauerkraut can breathe but mold cannot get inside."

"Uh, I don't think this cabbage is still alive," Eli said as I carefully set the lid into the groove around the top of the crock. "Not after we cut it up and pounded it. How can it breathe?"

"As the cabbage turns to sauerkraut, gases will form," Oma explained. "The gases float up around the lid, through the water in this channel—yes, pour it right in here, Hans Dieter—stop! Not so much it overflows! Yes, exactly like that."

"It's like a moat, but for sauerkraut," Eli said. "The lid sticks up out of it like a castle, and the sauerkraut waits down in the dungeon underneath."

"No, no, the sauerkraut is down in the treasure vault," Oma corrected. "The mold tries to break into the sauerkraut, but it cannot get in through the water."

Mom was telling Dad and Asad something in the other room, but I couldn't hear what she was saying, what with Eli and the ghost discussing what a mold-knight versus water-knight battle would look like.

"I want to see!" Asad yelled, and ran into the kitchen. Then he stopped.

Mom and Dad followed him in. Dad was looking around, but his eyes didn't stop on the ghost.

Asad looked right up at the ghost, who was floating next to me, waiting exactly like Mom had asked her to. "You don't look like my grandmom at all."

So, fine. Asad could see the ghost, and he wasn't freaking out the way I had when I first met her. Even my little brother would make a better Man in Black than I would. "That's because Grandmom Davis is Mom's mom, not Dad's mom. You probably don't remember Grandma Schenk, because she moved away before you were born, and you were really little last time we saw her," I told him. "Oma, this is my little brother, Asad Schenk."

"How nice to meet you, Asad," Oma said, smiling.

"We can call her Oma—it means 'grandma.' Although she's actually our great-great-grandma. Got it?" I said.

"How come she gets to use the food processor?" Asad wanted to know.

I frowned at him. "Just because she's a ghost doesn't mean she can't hear you, so be polite. She's a lot older than you, and she knows how to be responsible, and not put things in the food processor that she's not supposed to."

Dad was staring at us, like he didn't know what to say.

"Hi, Mr. Schenk," Eli said. "Do you smell anything?"

Dad sniffed. "Cabbage?"

"Anything sweet?" Eli asked.

Dad sniffed again. "Maybe?"

"Great job!" Eli said, making a note. "That's Mrs. S.'s violet soap."

"Can you hear me, Hans Peter?" the ghost said, very softly.

"Did you hear anything, Mr. Schenk?" Eli asked.

Dad shook his head, looking from Eli to me, to Asad, to Mom.

"It's okay, Dad," I told him. "Oma just said hello to you."

"Mrs. Schenk, could you please give Mrs. S. the pencil so she can say hello herself?" Eli asked Mom.

Mom held up the pencil and the notepad. She only flinched a tiny bit when Oma grabbed them. But, obviously, Mom's brave. She was a soldier.

Oma: Hello, Hans Peter. It is nice to meet you.

Dad's brave too, of course, same as Mom. He grabbed Mom's hand for a minute, but he didn't step back. And he only hesitated a little bit before he picked up the pencil that Oma had set down.

Dad: Nice to meet you too, Oma. My dad used to tell me stories about spending time with you when he was a kid.

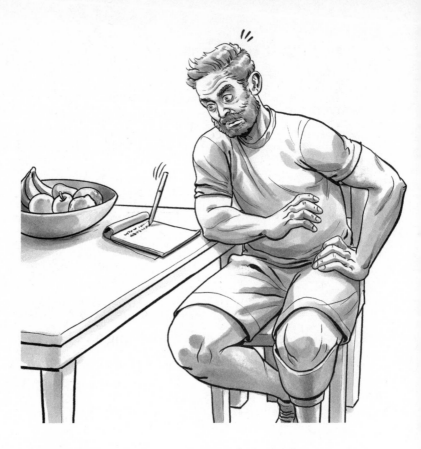

Oma: He remembered me? What did he
remember?

Dad: Well . . . I remember him telling me
about the cakes you used to bake.

Oma: My Gugelhupf! He did like that, yes.
But today we are making sauerkraut, not
cake. Which do you prefer: sauerkraut or
sauerruben?

Dad: What is sauerruben?

Oma: Your mother never made it? From turnips, instead of cabbage? You have this wonderful food processor and yet you do not make sauerruben?

Dad: Sorry. I guess not. My mother wasn't much of a cook.

Oma: Hans Dieter and Eli and I will make you some, after we finish the sauerkraut.

Dad: Thanks, I guess. It's nice to have you here, Great-Grandma. So—how long are you planning to stay?

Oma didn't bother to answer that one. Or maybe she didn't know.

"Come see what your brother and his friend have helped me make," Oma told Asad, floating over.

"Can you pick me up?" Asad asked the ghost.

"I don't think that's a good idea," Mom said, in the voice that means "no way, nohow."

"Here, check it out." I picked up Asad, and carefully lifted the lid. It made a burping noise when it came out of the water.

Asad giggled. "Excuse YOU, Grandma!"

Oma smiled and shook her head.

"Hey, Oma, there's more brine now," I told her, looking in.

Asad peered into the crock. "What is that going to be?"

Oma beamed. "It will be my famous sauerkraut! It will win the county fair!"

Asad sniffed it, and made a face. "I'm not eating that."

"Yeah, you might be too little to appreciate it," I said, and set him down. Something told me that Oma wasn't going to be telling Mom and Dad how helpful Asad was.

"Now, Hans Dieter, we must put a plate on top of the cabbage leaves—no, that one will not fit in the crock—yes, like that, and one more on top. Put it in— ah, yes, that will weigh them down, so the cabbage stays under the brine. . . ."

13

"So, what do you two have planned for tomorrow?" Mom asked as we sat down for dinner.

Oma grabbed her pencil, wrote something down, and held it up like a sign. *First we must check the brine, to make sure it covers the cabbage.*

I sighed. Another day of sauerkraut.

"Actually, I was talking to HD and Eli," Mom said, studying my face. "It's their first week of summer vacation, and, last I heard, they've got big plans. I'm sure they'll help you when they can, but you could probably check the brine on your own just this once, couldn't you?"

Oma grumbled a little, then wrote, *Very well.*

Huh. Maybe Aunt Nia had a point.

"What's on your list?" Mom asked again.

"I'm going to practice for my recital!" Eli said. "Ms. Izdebski's on vacation, so we have to practice on our own, and make our own costumes this year. HD said he'd help."

"And . . . ?" Mom asked him, eyebrows raised.

Eli thought for a minute. "And call my mom, between nine and noon!"

"Eli can call his mom, and then we can take the goats over to Maple Falls," I told Mom. "A scientist who studies crows is coming to speak, and Mr. Z. asked them to open the rec room doors so we see her from the lawn."

"I forgot about that," Eli said. "Awesome!"

"After that, we should probably take the goats to Uncle Gregor's with us," I said. "We can start working on their obstacle course, and then I can start on sorting out the basement, and Eli can practice his routine."

Dad nodded. "Some science, some fun, and some work—I like it. Just be home in time to do your chores before dinner."

"Eli, does that sound good to you?" Mom asked.

"It sounds great!" Eli said.

"I want to come too!" Asad wailed.

"You've got camp tomorrow, buddy," Dad said. "And then you promised Gloria and Ernie you'd draw some more pictures for the shop. Remember?"

Asad thought about that. "Okay," he said finally, still grumpy.

Mom turned to where Oma's pencil was floating. "Marietta, what are your plans for tomorrow?"

Oma underlined what she had already written, and held it up. "You will have time, before you leave," she told me, a little defensively.

I sighed. I was pretty sure it wouldn't end up being just one thing I had to help her with. Not with Oma and sauerkraut. But she was right, I could make time. "Okay, we'll help you first," I told her.

Dad looked at me. "Hey, Oma, Asad and I missed out on helping you make the sauerkraut. Could we help you check the brine tomorrow?"

Oma looked surprised, then a little uncertain. *Yes, thank you,* she wrote at last.

Dad nodded. "We'll do that before I take Asad to camp, then. Will you be okay all day while we're gone?" He hesitated. "HD, should we leave the TV on or something?"

But Oma was already writing again. *I will go with HD.*

"Uh, Mrs. S., that might be kind of tricky, now that

your crock is all full of sauerkraut," Eli said. "What if it fell over and spilled?"

Then we would make sauerkraut again, Oma wrote. *I have spent more than fifty years alone. Now I want to spend time with my grandson.*

"You mean your great-great-grandson," Eli pointed out.

"Maybe we should let HD and Eli do their own thing tomorrow," Mom said. "We'll see them at dinner, after all."

But I was thinking it over. Oma had been lonely for a long time. It wasn't anybody's fault, but I still felt bad for her. Would taking her along stop me from doing my thing? Not really, I decided—at least, not if we left on time.

Some superheroes have handlers—people who make things work smoothly for them in the world. Like the Avengers had Nick Fury and Agent Coulson and Agent Hill. I guess Oma had already decided that I would be her handler.

Maybe I wasn't the only person who could see the ghost. Maybe I freaked out some when I first met her—more than Asad did, anyway. (Although he hadn't met her in Uncle Gregor's spooky basement, and he had a heads-up first. I like to think I'd have done better under those conditions too.) But I got over it, and did my research, and I'd had a lot of practice helping her since then, figuring out her Grand Purpose and making sauerkraut. So maybe I was the right person for the job after all.

"Okay," I told her. "You can come too."

The next morning, Mom went to work, and Dad made pancakes for us. Then he and Asad helped Oma check the sauerkraut while Eli called his mom and I figured out how to take a crock full of sauerkraut with us to Maple Falls.

First I thought about what my design needed to do: get a heavy crock to Maple Falls without falling over, sloshing, spilling, or rattling around.

Next I gathered my supplies and tools: the wagon, a bunch of towels, masking tape, two bungee cords, the old hammock, some string, a pair of scissors, and a clean water bottle.

After that I went to see how Dad and Asad and Oma were doing.

Just in time too. "What's sauerruben?" Asad asked.

"We will make it! All we will need is some turnips, and another box of salt—"

"Hey, Oma, do you still want to come?" I asked. (I

know interrupting is rude, but it would be impossible to wait until Oma was done discussing sauerkraut, and sauer- everything else.)

"Yes, I will go with you," Oma said, floating over.

"Okay," I said. "Dad, can you bring Oma's crock out to the wagon for me?"

Sometimes people think Dad can't lift heavy stuff, or drive, or do much of anything since he lost part of his leg. But Dad's really strong, and Mom says he went right back to working out once he got his new leg fitted. He has a special leg that can handle all the heavy stuff he has to lift at the auto body shop, so Oma's crock was no big deal for him. Uncle Gregor said he should train up and try out for the Paralympics. But Dad told him he has his hands full with the shop and all of us right now. Too bad; it would have been cool to go see him compete.

Dad set the crock in the wagon. "Are you going to be able to get this out again safely?"

I bent my knees and tried lifting the crock. It was heavy when it was empty, and it was way heavier full. The handles wouldn't make it easy for me and Eli to lift it together either. "Oma, you might have to stay in the kitchen at Uncle Gregor's, with the wagon—I'm not sure I can carry your crock all the way down to the basement. Are you okay with that?"

"Yes," Oma said. "I never wish to see that basement again. Does Gregor make sauerkraut?"

"We're good," I told Dad.

He nodded, and helped me pack the towels around the crock, tape the lid down so it wouldn't bounce, and wrap bungee cords around the neck of the crock, hooking them over the sides of the wagon. I tied the hammock over the top, and Dad jostled the wagon to see if everything was secure, then gave me a thumbs-up. "What's the water for?" he asked.

"In case the water in the moat sloshes out," I told him. "That way we can refill it, hopefully before any mold spores get in."

"Done!" Eli said, shutting the door behind him.

"How's your mom doing?" Dad asked. "Did you tell her about, er, our guest?"

"She's good," Eli said. "Yeah, I told her, but she just said I have an astonishing imagination." He shrugged and smiled. "Once she gets home and Mrs. S. can write to her, she'll see."

Dad looked relieved. "Great. Anything else you two need before Asad and I head out? HD, you've got your keys, right?"

"Yeah, Dad," I said, patting my pocket. "We're good. Really."

It was a beautiful morning—not too hot, not too cool. People say it always rains near Seattle, and yeah, it rains, but not every day. The goats were ready for some exercise, so after they tried to knock each other off their playhouse, they came over and let Oma and Eli pet them while I clipped their leashes onto their collars.

It doesn't take long to get to Maple Falls, even with goats trying to jump in your wagon and a ghost shooing them out and telling them to behave. A few people stared at us, but that might have been the goats, not Oma. They didn't stop driving, so we couldn't ask.

"Guess what, Mr. Z.?" Eli yelled across the lawn.

"HD glued the lid back together, and I can see the ghost now too!" He and Rodgers jogged over to Mr. Z.'s chair, and Rodgers stuck his face in Mr. Z.'s bag of carrot sticks.

Hammerstein strained toward Mr. Z., and I pulled the wagon and followed him over.

"*Hallo*," I said, nodding to Mr. Z. "The silicone sealant worked great, thanks."

"*Hallo*, HD. *Hallo*, Eli," Mr. Z. said, nudging Rodgers's face out of the bag so he could give Hammerstein a carrot stick too. "I am glad to hear it." He stood up and leaned over the crock, examining the lid. "Yes, very good work, HD."

"Mrs. S. wanted to come too," Eli explained. "We already made her sauerkraut, so we have to be careful not to spill it, but she didn't want to stay home by herself."

"It is a pleasure to see—er, to spend time with you again, Mrs. Schenk," Mr. Z. said. "HD, I believe Ms. Stevermer will be attending the lecture today. Perhaps Mrs. Schenk would like to meet her?"

"Who?" Eli asked.

"The writer who collects ghost stories," I told him. "That would be great. Oma, you'd like to meet her, wouldn't you?"

"Does she make sauerkraut?" Oma asked.

"I think you should ask her that yourself," I told her.

Mr. Z. checked his watch. "Shall we see if she has arrived, then, and find our seats?"

So we followed Mr. Z. to the chairs they'd set out for us, where we'd have a good view of the presentation through the open doors, away from the petunias.

Mr. Z. went into the rec room. He came back with Ms. Stevermer, followed by the older lady who'd been asleep last time. Both were carrying plastic chairs.

The older lady put her chair down on the lawn, sat down carefully, and promptly fell asleep.

Ms. Stevermer put her chair down too, and Hammerstein head-butted it. It fell over. I set it back up for her. "Nice to see you again."

"And you as well," she said as Rodgers climbed up into her chair. She looked over at the crock. "Have you brought your great-great-grandmother to see the presentation? That was very thoughtful."

"She wanted to come," Eli said, lifting Rodgers down. He stuck his hand out. "I'm Eli. Hey, Mrs. S., did you bring your pencil?"

Ms. Stevermer shook his hand. "Ah, very clever! Perhaps I have one here. . . ." She rummaged around in her purse, brought out a metal pencil box shaped like a sarcophagus, and opened it.

Hammerstein butted Mr. Z.'s hand, to see if he had any more carrot sticks. Mr. Z. handed him one, then took Rodgers's lead from Eli, who was helping Ms. Stevermer and Oma get to know each other, and led the way over to the chairs.

We sat down, and Mr. Z. gave Rodgers another carrot stick too. "How is your project coming along, HD?"

"Well, I haven't got much done yet—we've been busy helping Oma make her sauerkraut," I told him. "But we're going to Uncle Gregor's after this. Eli and I want to start setting up the GOAT Obstacle Course, and Eli has his recital to practice and his solo to figure out, and I need to sort out Uncle Gregor's basement, so I can buy my components." I sighed. "I don't know. . . . It just feels like a lot right now."

"I see," Mr. Z. said, nodding. "This is a complex situation. And what do complex situations call for?"

"A plan," I said.

He nodded. "Now, focus on one project. Say, building your computer. What is the goal?"

I sat up in my chair a little straighter. "I want to build my own computer from scratch, with money I earn myself, and enter it into the county fair so everyone can see what I can do."

"Excellent," Mr. Z. said. "What are your resources?"

"Well, we've got three of the best minds in the business working on this problem: you, me, and Eli," I said, starting to feel a little better. (Mr. Z. always says our minds are our best tools for any job.) "I've got a job so I can earn the money, and Mom and Dad said I could spend most days at Uncle Gregor's until I'm done sorting things, as long as I check in." We both know time is an important resource too.

"Very good," Mr. Z. said. "I wonder if perhaps you have a new resource now too?" He nodded at Oma's crock.

I hesitated. "I think Oma knows more about sauerkraut than computers."

"You may be right," he said. "But perhaps she knows the things you are sorting, if they came from her family?"

"Maybe," I said. "Grace said I could come make a list of exactly which components I want, and how much they cost, and she'd help me make sure they'll all work together. So when I've sorted through half the boxes, I'm going to go do that."

"How many boxes are there?" Mr. Z. asked.

"Fifty-two," I told him with a sigh. "I only have to do the boxes, not the chain saws and furniture and stuff. But it's still going to be a while. In the meantime, Harry's been saving articles on computer builds for me, and I'm making a list of the steps we talked about too."

Mr. Z. smiled at me. "A solid plan, and one that will work well, I think."

"I hope so," I said, throwing a carrot stick up in the air for Rodgers to catch.

"I think she's starting," Eli hissed, and we all got ready for the crow scientist's presentation. Eli and I made notes and everything.

FACTS ABOUT CROWS, ACCORDING TO THE CROW SCIENTIST:

• They use tools.

• When walnuts get ripe, they put them in driveways so cars will run over them and crack them open.

• When someone messes with a baby crow, they tell the whole neighborhood of crows about it, and then every time that person goes anywhere, they get yelled at by crows they haven't even met.

• They protect other crows, even against eagles and other birds way bigger than they are.

- Someone did an experiment where different
  people wore the same mask on different days and
  the crows recognized it. When one of them wore
  the mask upside down, the crows turned their
  heads upside down to check it out! (How do you
  even wear a mask upside down? Do you have to
  cut more holes in it or something? Mr. Z. said we
  could ask her afterward, but she was already gone
  when we got Rodgers and Hammerstein untangled
  from my chair.)

Afterward, Ms. Stevermer came over to me. "HD, it has been such a pleasure, communicating with your great-great-grandmother! Thank you for introducing us." She hesitated. "She has invited me to continue our discussion at your uncle's house, but I thought that I should check with you or your parents, to be certain that's okay."

Oma floated over. "HD, I am going to teach Ms. Stevermer how to make sauerkraut!"

Mr. Z. cleared his throat. "Perhaps I could call your father, HD, and if he agrees, I could come also. Then Ms. Stevermer and I could both visit with your oma while you work."

That seemed reasonable. "What do you think, Oma? Is it okay if Mr. Z. comes too?"

142

"Yes, yes," Oma said, rushing back for her pencil.

"She says that's fine," I told Mr. Z.

"Very good," he said. "Then, if your father agrees, we will meet you at your uncle's house in one hour? And if he feels a different day would be better, I will call and let you know."

"That works," I told him. If we left now, we'd have time to walk there, get the goats settled, roll Oma inside, and have lunch before they arrived. And find some more pencils.

By the time they got to Uncle Gregor's house, Eli and I had eaten our sandwiches and drawn some plans for the GOAT Obstacle Course. I took Mr. Z. out back to show him where we're going to build the course, and he approved the first couple of steps of our project plan and gave me some more ideas.

Eli got Ms. Stevermer a glass of water, and Oma shared her pencils and paper.

Then Eli and I went downstairs to work, and left them to it.

It was funny: Uncle Gregor's basement wasn't spooky at all anymore. Eli said that was because it wasn't haunted now: We'd already met the ghost and now she was upstairs haunting the kitchen instead.

But I felt like it wasn't so much about her, really. It was something about me, and how I saw things now.

All those dusty boxes of cookbooks and paint cans and nylons with a hole in them were just sad, stuck down there where no one could use them. But I knew I could fix all that, eventually.

After an hour or so, I had sorted a whole stack of boxes into piles, and Eli had done his routine almost perfectly two times in a row. We took a break for Popsicles.

"Mrs. Schenk, is your pickling crock a family heirloom?" Ms. Stevermer was asking.

No, it is new, Oma wrote. *My grandson chose it for my birthday. We were going to make sauerkraut together.*

"Wait, what? I thought you made sauerkraut all the time!" I said.

Yes, but in an old crock, not nearly so nice, Oma wrote.

"I see . . ." Ms. Stevermer looked up from her notes. She studied me for a moment, then closed her notebook. "Thank you for introducing me to your oma," she told me. "It's been quite fascinating."

"I'm glad we could help you with your research," I told her.

"I wish you the best of success with your sauerkraut, and whatever the future holds for you," Ms. Stevermer told Oma's pencil. "Do let me know if you have time to talk again."

Certainly, Oma wrote. *And after we make sauerkraut, we can make sauerruben!*

"I'm afraid I really must be going, though. You're sure I can't give you a lift?" Ms. Stevermer asked Mr. Z.

"No thank you," he said. "I will call Eleanora when we're done visiting."

As she left, I put the box I was carrying on the kitchen table. "Oma, could you tell me if these are important or not?"

"In a minute . . . ," she said, still writing something to Mr. Z.

I pulled the first thing out of the box, and she looked up, then crowded over to see. "My apron!" she cried, and hugged the faded cloth.

I grinned; Mr. Z. had been right, sort of. Maybe that old apron wasn't a treasure to anyone else, but it was to my oma. I knew which pile it was going into now.

"What about these?" I asked, holding up two rolling pins.

Oma examined them. "This one is mine—it is perfect for cookies! That one I've never seen before. Probably it would not work well."

I nodded. "Okay, what about these? Do you know who any of these people are?" I held up a stack of photos.

Oma snatched up the top one, and sank slowly down near her crock, staring at it.

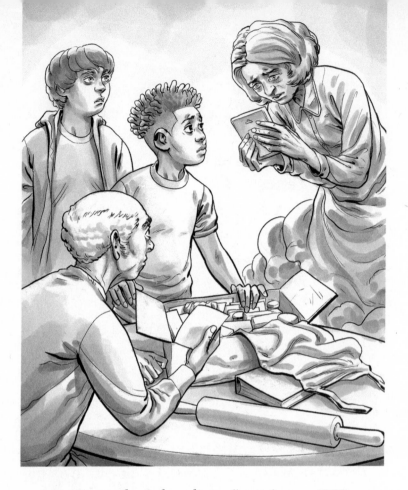

Mr. Z. watched the photo float down. "HD, perhaps your oma and I will make a list of these photos
together," he said quietly. "When she is ready."

"Okay!" Eli said. "Can we go start the obstacle
course now?"

"Oma, are you okay?" I asked her.

Slowly she nodded, smiling, even though I could
see the ghost tears on her cheeks. "Go, go, have fun,"
she said.

So Eli and I went out to the backyard and climbed Uncle Gregor's plum tree so we could hang a Hula Hoop from it. We tied a couple more pieces of rope onto the hoop, and tied the other ends to a couple of sticks we stuck into the lawn, like Mr. Z. suggested. That way, it wouldn't spin around while the goats were trying to go through it.

Rodgers and Hammerstein got the idea right away, once I brought out the rest of Mr. Z.'s carrots sticks. They didn't like taking turns, but luckily the Hula Hoop was big enough for them to both go through at once.

After that, we dragged over some cement blocks and a long board and built a balance beam. The goats

jumped right up on it, but they were more interested in knocking each other off of it than walking across it.

We went inside to see what Mr. Z. thought. He and Oma had finished their photo list, and Oma looked happier again. We wheeled her out back so they could see what we'd been working on.

After we convinced Hammerstein that I had the treats, not Oma or Mr. Z., they did a pretty good job of following my hand and showing off their moves.

"You are off to a wonderful start!" Mr. Z. said, patting Hammerstein's head when he came back over to make extra certain Mr. Z. didn't have anything for him.

"We're going to make the seesaw next," Eli said. "You should come again and see them try it out!"

"Perhaps I will," Mr. Z. said, smiling. "But for now, I should call Eleanora, and you had better get home for dinner."

So Oma helped Eli get the goats rounded up again, while I went over our seesaw plans with Mr. Z. until Eleanora came to pick him up.

Before he left, he wrote out a note, folded it up, and handed it to me. "For Mrs. Schenk," he said. "When you are home."

I nodded. "Thanks for helping her with the photos."

"The list is there, along with the photos. I am glad she was a resource after all," Mr. Z. said.

"Yeah, you were right. *Danke*," I told him. (That means "thank you.")

He smiled. "*Gern geschehen*, my friend." (That means "my pleasure.")

After he left, I went back into the basement. I put the rolling pin that wasn't Oma's in the "someone else could use this" pile, and got the frame and the index card I'd found, along with Oma's apron and rolling pin and photos and list.

"Hey, Oma," I said. "I thought you might want this for one of your photos. And I found this too." I held the frame and the card out to her.

Slowly she floated over in front of me. She reached out and touched the fancy edge of the frame. "It is perfect." Then she took the card from my hand and read it. "Hans Dieter, you have found my cherry kuchen recipe!" She swooped down and gave me a hug.

This time, I didn't flinch. I just stood there and smiled, and hugged her back. "I bet I can find the rest of your stuff too." Then we packed everything up into the wagon and headed for home.

When we got there, I gave her Mr. Z.'s note, like he asked me to.

Sehr geehrte Frau Schenk,

We both know that your grandson HD is a brilliant young man, full of ideas, as well as a kind young man. He is working on a number of projects this summer, and it is my pleasure to assist him. I would like to offer my assistance to you too if I may, or, at least my company. Please let me know if you would like me to come and visit with you again one of these days.

Mit freundlichen Grüßen,
Matthias Ziedrich

PS If you should ever meet Mrs. Annegret Ziedrich, here, or wherever you might find yourself, please,

tell her I will always love her, and that I miss her
every day.

The next day, Oma had a discussion with my mom about how to explain to Mr. Z. that she didn't know any other ghosts, let alone his wife. Once they sorted that out, Oma decided she'd invite Mr. Z. over for a visit while Eli and I did our own thing.

Eli and I were working on some ghostly research when he arrived.

"I cannot reach it," Oma said, straining toward the door as the doorbell rang again.

"Be right there," Eli yelled as I measured the distance between her crock and her position. "Fourteen feet, one and a quarter inches," I told Eli, and he nodded and wrote it down.

I went to get the door.

It was Mr. Z., carrying a bag and a travel mug of coffee.

"Sorry, we were testing out Oma's range," I told him. "Come on in."

"It's like she has a ghostly leash," Eli said. "Hi, Mr. Z.! What's that?"

Mr. Z. handed me the bag, smiling. "Something Mrs. Schenk might recognize."

Inside were four pieces of poppy-seed cake. "Thanks," I said, and went to get some plates and forks.

Oma floated over to where we'd set up her photos, the frame, some glass cleaner, and a rag on the table, and cleared some space.

"Mom and Dad decided we should make a photo wall," I explained, putting the plates on the table. "We each get to pick some of our favorite photos for it." I took a bite of cake. "Did you make this?" I asked Mr. Z. It was pretty good, for plain poppy-seed cake.

"No, it is from the bakery," he told me. "I never learned to make my oma's recipes."

Oma poked at her piece with her fork, and sniffed it. *It is probably good,* she wrote after a minute. *But not as good as mine.*

"Oma!" I whispered. "Be polite!"

Mr. Z. laughed. "Not as good as my oma's either, I'm afraid. But perhaps you will teach us how to make yours someday?"

Oma looked at me, and smiled.

I stuffed the last of the cake into my mouth. "Eli, we'd better get going," I said. "Bye, Oma! Mr. Z., do you want to come say hi to Rodgers and Hammerstein before we take them to the obstacle course?" We had a lot to do today, and none of it involved baking cakes.

Instead, we spent our morning sorting boxes, tap-dancing at the top of Eli's lungs, and picking up more computer articles and comics from the library. And no one interrupted us to talk about sauerkraut at all.

After lunch, I emptied out the perfect box, so Eli started building his costume. He's going to be one of the skyscrapers tap-dancing to *42nd Street* for his recital at the fair, and he has to make up a special solo for eight beats.

ELI'S SKYSCRAPER COSTUME

NEED:

1 Eli-sized box (not so tall it will scrape on the ground, but not so short that his whole legs stick out and look dumb, either)

black spray paint

chalk

tinfoil

glue

box cutter

STEPS:

Spray-paint box black. Wait for box to dry.

Try box on. Measure where eyeholes go. Mark with chalk. Take box off.

When a non-ghostly adult is present, carefully cut square eyeholes with the box cutter.

Draw evenly spaced chalk lines for where you want the bottoms of the windows to go.

Cut up lots of tinfoil windows.

Stick tinfoil windows in rows along the lines.

Rub off the chalk lines.

Test out your skyscraper costume with some cool moves!

"We should cut out some armholes," I told him.

"That's what I thought too," Eli said. "But Ms. Iz-debski said you still can't move your arms enough to be useful, and it looks better this way. Plus, she says you need to hold the box steady from the inside so it doesn't roll around on your head."

We measured to find out what part of Eli's arms could stick out of the box, but his teacher was right: the box was going to get in the way.

"I don't know, man. This looks tough to dance in," I told him.

But Eli just smiled. "That's why we're starting

now, so I have time to practice in it. You should see the advanced-level costumes!"

While Eli put on Uncle Gregor's coveralls and gloves and sprayed the box, I read the articles Harry had found for me about how to build a computer, and thought about the games I wanted to put on it. Then we decided it was time to work on the seesaw.

HD AND ELI'S GOAT OBSTACLE COURSE: THE SEESAW

SUPPLIES:

One cylindrical log (about 10 to 12 inches in diameter)

One wide board (about 8 inches wide and 8 feet long)

Eight 3-inch deck screws

TOOLS:

Measuring tape

Pencil

Safety goggles

Drill

Drill bit that's a little smaller around than your screws

Screwdriver bit that fits your screws

STEPS:

1. Measure the length of the board and make a line across the middle with a pencil. Measure and mark two more lines across the board an inch away from the middle, on either side.

2. Do a dry run: Lift the board up so that the middle of the board is on top of the log.

3. Use your common sense to evaluate your design: Is the end of the seesaw sticking up so high that a goat could fall off of it and get hurt? Could a goat on the lower end get catapulted into the sky if someone jumped up on it?

4. Ask a responsible adult who is not a ghost to supervise so you can use the drill.

5. Put the board on a flat surface. Put your safety goggles on. Put the drill bit into the drill.

6. Drill four holes along each line on either side of the middle of the board.

7. Have someone hold the board in place on top of the log. Carefully drill through the holes you already drilled and into the log. (Watch out for goats—they like to come see what you're up to.)

8. Take out the drill bit and put in the screwdriver bit. Carefully screw the board onto the log.

9. Wiggle the board and make sure it's secure.

10. Stand back, and let the goats try it out!

Mr. Z. came over to supervise our drilling and box-cutting. When Rodgers and Hammerstein jumped on the seesaw, he said he'd probably never laughed that hard in his life, and that he admired our inventive young minds.

When we got home, we found out that Mr. Z. had taught Oma about the History Channel, so she could catch up on the world, and Oma had sent Mr. Z. to pick things up at the store for her, and had baked her cherry kuchen.

"Now we will have a kaffeeklatsch!" she said, beaming.

"Um, I'm not supposed to drink coffee," Eli said. "But whatever that is smells really good."

"Sorry, Oma—Mom's going to be mad if we have dessert right before dinner," I said. "House rules."

Oma frowned, but she didn't argue. At least, not

after Mom came home and explained the dessert rules to her.

So after dinner, Oma served us all pieces of her cherry kuchen on Mom's special plates.

Dad was the first one to take a bite. He closed his eyes and stopped chewing.

"Do you need to spit it out, Mr. Schenk?" Eli asked him, putting his fork down.

"Spit out my Kirschenkuchen?" Oma asked, glaring at Eli.

Dad opened his eyes and smiled. "No, no—it's delicious. It reminds me of my aunt's kuchen. I haven't tasted it since she died." Dad's eyes looked kind of like he might cry, even though he was still smiling.

Oma settled back, and patted his hand. *Perhaps hers was good too*, she wrote. *But I will teach you how to make mine.*

Dad nodded. "I'd like that, Oma."

"You better learn fast, though," Eli told him.

"Why is that?" Dad asked.

"We think Oma's going to level up at the fair, remember?" I told Dad. "She might not be around after that." I got kind of a lump in my throat when I said it.

Dad looked like maybe he did too.

After we finished our kuchen (it was pretty good—like cake with cherries on top), Oma handed Dad the photo she'd picked out. Mr. Z. had helped her frame it.

"How about here?" Dad asked, holding it up in the middle of the wall.

Oma studied it carefully, then nodded at me, so I told Dad to go ahead.

"Would you tell us about the photo you chose?" Mom asked her while Dad got out the hammer and one of the special art hangers he'd brought home.

Oma picked up her pencil. *This is a photo of my grandson, Hans Gerhard, when he was six years old. A neighbor girl had a camera, and Hans Gerhard begged her to take a photograph of him.*

I stared at the photo. My granddad—Oma's grandson—was just a little kid, giggling at the camera like Asad does. The lady sitting next to him had her arm around him. She was smiling at the camera.

"Is that you, Oma?" Dad asked.

Oma nodded. *Yes. Every day, after school, we would take a walk together, and then we would have a kaffeeklatsch: cocoa for him, coffee for me, and something sweet, and we would tell each other about our days. My Kirschenkuchen was his favorite.*

"You must really miss him," Mom said quietly.

Yes, Oma wrote. *Now, who would like more kuchen?*

After that, Mom and Oma came to an agreement: We could have a kaffeeklatsch with Oma in the afternoons when we got home, as long as it was a small piece of something not too sugary, with milk, not cocoa, at least two hours before dinner.

"If you write us a list, we'll pick up whatever ingredients you need," Dad told her. "And I would prefer that another adult is home when you use the oven or stove."

I have been cooking since before you were born, Oma wrote, frowning.

"Yeah, but what if there was a fire, and your sauerkraut burned up because nine-one-one couldn't hear you?" Eli asked.

"And your photos and everything?" I added. "And our house?"

Very well, Oma wrote. *Hans Dieter, I will need you to find some of my things for me.*

So we made a list.

FIND FOR OMA:

Recipe cards

Two square cake pans

Gugelhupf pan (kind of like a Bundt pan, with a hole in the middle, but Oma says Mom's Bundt pan won't work, she needs hers instead)

Batter bowl (a big green glass bowl with a handle)

Poppy-seed grinder (has a handle that turns)

And we must invite Mr. Ziedrich again tomorrow, she wrote.

"I have an idea for how you can do that, Oma. Do you know how to type?" I asked.

"Of course I can type," Oma said. "You have found a typewriter for me?"

I smiled. "Not exactly . . . Mom and Dad, can I help Oma get her own email address?"

16

I did at least an hour of sorting every day, after we took the goats to see Mr. Z. Then Eli worked on his recital dance and especially on his solo. (I think he comes up with a new version every single day.)

Sorting out Uncle Gregor's basement didn't go fast, because there were a LOT of boxes. But it wasn't really hard either. I mean, maybe somebody can use four bags of sweaters with fake pearl buttons, but Mom said not her, and Oma said she never gets cold anymore, and Eli said it might freak people out to see a sweater flying around anyway, like it surprised Dad when she forgot to take her apron off and came to say hi. So I knew which pile to put all those in.

I labeled a new pile too: stuff to ask Oma about. I put all the kitchen stuff in there, and all the photos, and anything with old handwriting that was hard to read. That way, I wouldn't give anything she really wanted away by accident.

Mom stopped by a couple of times to pick up bags and bags of clothes with no holes or anything, to take to a place out near the farms she works with. (You don't give people stuff that's already trashed, because that's not respectful.) And Dad took the boxes of records and fourteen lamps to the Maple Falls thrift store on his lunch break. After that, we had a LOT more space to work.

Then, when we got hungry or bored, we made some lunch, and worked on Eli's costume and my computer notes, and on the GOAT Obstacle Course, and read, and thought up more ghost research to try during our kaffeeklatsch.

Oma stayed home and got ready for our kaffeeklatsch. Mr. Ziedrich came over most days before we got back, so Oma could bake stuff, and sometimes Oma invited Ms. Stevermer too.

I have to say, kaffeeklatsches are a pretty good invention. I kept Mr. Z. up to date on how my projects were going, and Eli tried out his solos before a test audience. We filled Oma and Mr. Z. in on the comics we were reading, and Mr. Z. shared what he'd been reading about new inventions and scientific discoveries and some pretty cool projects we might build someday. And of course Oma told us all about how the sauerkraut was doing. (Pretty good, I guess, even though it just sat in the crock smelling like old socks. At least, it wasn't moldy.)

Ms. Stevermer always asked how our ghost research was coming along. So we shared our notes with her, about how far Oma could go from her crock, and how we'd proven that the goats could hear her and see her, and what happened when Oma took a bite of something (it fell straight through her mouth and onto the floor, and Oma said she couldn't even taste it), and how long Oma could hold her breath if she stuck her face in the bathroom sink when it was full of water (we all got bored after twenty minutes). We told her our theory that maybe our ages had something to do with why we could see Oma and no one else could. She thought we should explore that further, when we had time.

I'd found a couple more of Oma's recipes, so she made these moon-shaped almond cookies that were pretty good. And I found her bowl with the handle, and she decided she liked Mom's cake pans better than hers anyway. But I hadn't found her special gugelhupf pan or her poppy-seed grinder yet. (I thought I did the other day, but it turned out to be somebody else's meat grinder, and Oma said no way, we definitely could not give that a try with her poppy seeds, so that went back to the pile that somebody else could use. And we already tried putting poppy seeds in the food processor. Didn't work.)

When we were done catching up, Mr. Z. asked Oma a lot of questions about her family, and saved all the answers in a stack for us.

I caught Dad reading them in the kitchen one day after dinner while Oma was playing checkers with Asad in the family room, and Eli was doing hockey-style announcing for them.

Dad saw me, and put the page down with a smile.

"You know you could ask her stuff too," I told him. "She loves to talk about her family."

Dad nodded. "You're right, I should. I was just thinking . . . Do you remember your grandma Schenk?"

"Not really," I told him. "She didn't make sauerkraut, did she?"

Dad shook his head. "Nah, she was interested in other stuff. I wish I could have asked her some of these things before she died, though. Then I could tell you and Asad more about her."

"Sorry, Dad—I think if she was in the basement, Oma or I would have run into her by now. Tell you what, though: I'll find a binder, and we can make a section for Oma, and a section for Grandma Schenk, and maybe Grandpa Schenk and Great-Aunt Gerta too, and you can write down whatever you do know," I said.

Dad smiled, even though he still looked kind of sad. He reached out and gave me a hug. "That's a great idea. And who knows, maybe your uncle remembers some stories about them."

We still got to have dessert after dinner too, so we could keep up with everything Oma baked. Asad begged her to make brownies, but she just smiled and told him she'd make something he would love. (She made him something called zwieback that she said was a cookie, but it looked more like a cracker, and kind of tasted like one. It had raisins. It didn't go well.)

In the sixteenth box, I found another frame.

Mom got to pick the next photo for our wall. It was of her in her fancy wedding dress, sitting on Dad's lap at their wedding. Uncle Gregor is pretending to push Dad's wheelchair at the camera person, and Grandmom and Grandpop Davis and Aunt Nia are all laughing.

Mom told us about how she and Dad had been talking about getting married when their army contracts were up. When Dad got injured right before then, they decided to do it as soon as he got out of the hospital, even before he got used to his new leg.

"I told your dad I was not going to sit on the sidelines at my own wedding, though," Mom said, laughing. "So I danced every single dance in that ridiculous dress—with your aunt Nia, your uncle Gregor, my parents, and all our friends."

"Didn't you get bored watching everyone else dance?" Eli asked Dad.

Dad shook his head. "I could have watched her all night," he said, smiling. "Besides, she saved all the slow dances for me."

"Dance with me too!" Asad said, and Mom and Dad laughed and led him into the kitchen, where there was more room for dancing.

Oma floated over to where Eli and I were sitting. "Did my grandson come to the wedding?" she asked, still looking at Mom's photo.

"Nah, Grandpa Schenk died before they got married, when Mom and Dad were in the army and Uncle Gregor was still in school," I told her. "Mom only met him once or twice, when they were on leave."

Oma stared from Mom's photo to hers, and back again. Maybe she was crying, or maybe her eyes were just glowing more than usual.

The day I finished sorting the twenty-sixth box in Uncle Gregor's basement, I found Oma's special gugelhupf pan and poppy-seed grinder in a box with a bunch of *National Geographic* magazines. I took them all out and shook them, and a recipe card fell out, for something called Mohngugelhupf. I put the magazines in the pile that someone else could use, and packed the rest up to give to Oma at our kaffeeklatsch.

"This is wonderful, Hans Dieter!" Oma cried, swooping in to give me a ghostly kiss on the forehead. She stuck her ghostly fingers into the poppy-seed grinder. A few very dusty poppy seeds fell out the bottom.

"Careful, Oma!" I told her. "I bet that thing could take your finger right off."

"Wait, did you have to flatten out your fingers or something to get them in there?" Eli wanted to know, opening his notebook. "Could you stick your finger through these fork prongs so I can see how it works?"

"Perhaps I could clean that for you," Mr. Z. said.

Oma floated the poppy-seed grinder over and dropped it in Mr. Z.'s hands. "Tomorrow we can make my Mohngugelhupf!"

"Actually, Eli and I are going to Rose's RadioJunk-YardBirds tomorrow," I told her. "I need to make a list of exactly what components I'm buying for my project."

"That can wait," Oma said. "Tomorrow is Mohngugelhupf day! You will love it as much as my grandson did."

I hesitated. I didn't want to hurt Oma's feelings, but I wasn't sure how to tell her I really wanted to do my plan, not hers.

"I bet we will, Mrs. S.! Well, unless it has raisins in it," Eli said. "But we can't help you tomorrow, because this is the next step of HD's plan, and we have to keep him on track for the fair. You know how that goes."

Oma's ghostly form drooped a little. "But . . . I wanted to bake this with him."

"Sorry, Oma, but Eli's right," I said. "I could help

you the next day, though." It might get me a little off track on the basement project, but I could probably catch up, if I skipped the obstacle course for a couple of days.

Mr. Z. came back in, drying off the pieces of the poppy-seed grinder with a dish towel. "I haven't used one of these since I was a boy, helping my oma."

Oma grabbed her pencil. *Tell Hans Dieter how much he will love helping me tomorrow,* she wrote, and shoved the paper at Mr. Z.

Slowly he set the pieces down, and picked up the paper, looking at my face.

"HD finished box twenty-six today." Eli opened my notebook and showed him the steps of my plan. "We're supposed to go to Rose's tomorrow and make a list."

"Ah, I see," Mr. Z. said.

"Well, I do not see," Oma muttered.

Mr. Z. settled back into his chair and tapped his fingers together thoughtfully. "The first time I tasted Mohngugelhupf, I knew it was magic," he said at last. "We were visiting my oma—yes, for kaffeeklatsch—and she took the pan out of the oven. I could not imagine what could make that glorious smell!"

"Yes, yes!" Oma said. "And Hans Dieter—"

Mr. Z. couldn't hear her, though, so he kept talking.

"But I did not help her make that first cake. Sometimes we fall in love with the magic, before we learn more."

Oma got quiet. *Perhaps.*

"Would you let me help you, this time?" Mr. Z. asked. "I would like one more turn with a poppy-seed grinder."

Oma looked at me, and I held my breath.

Just this once, she wrote at last.

I let my breath out, and grinned at Eli.

I'd found another frame, so that night it was Dad's turn to pick a photo. He picked one from when Asad was born, when we went to visit Mom in the hospital. Mom's still in her hospital outfit, looking tired, but she's smiling, and Dad is grinning and has his arm around her. I don't look too sure about things, and Asad is screaming his head off.

Will you tell us about this photo? Oma wrote.

Dad nodded, clearing his throat. "I've had a lot of happy days in my life, but this was one of the happiest," he said. Then he stopped, and had to wipe his eyes.

"That's because you didn't have to do the hard part," Mom said, laughing. She hugged him while he got himself back together.

Then he cleared his throat again. "Of all the things I've done here on this earth, I'm proudest of you boys, and of being your dad."

Trust Asad to ruin Dad's moment. "We're loud! We're proud! We're gonna take off and fly in a cloud!" he yelled, running around the family room. "And . . . TACKLE!" He grabbed Oma around the waist and tried to tackle her to the ground. Good thing I was there to catch him.

After Mom and Dad calmed Asad down again and went to get the kitchen squared away, Oma floated over to me. "Did your oma take care of you when your brother was born?"

"You mean Grandma Schenk?" I shook my head. "She moved to Arizona to help her sister a few years after Grandpa Schenk died. Mom says some people have a hard time staying in a place where everything reminds them of someone they've lost. But Uncle Gregor took care of me while Dad took Mom to the hospital, and Grandmom and Grandpop Davis came up to help us out, so we were fine."

Oma was shaking her head. "No, no—you cannot move. You cannot leave everything behind. . . . What if you forget?"

I shrugged. "I guess she was ready to move on."

The next morning, Eli and I rode our bikes to Rose's RadioJunkYardBirds, right after we fed the goats and helped Oma check on her sauerkraut. (Maybe it was a little less stinky.)

I nodded at Grace, behind the counter.

She nodded back. "Hey, HD. Hey, Eli. You want to see something?"

"Yeah, I'm here to start making my list," I told her.

Grace smiled. "You're getting close, huh? You got it. Where do you want to start?"

"Let's start with the CPU," I said.

CPU: $99.99

Motherboard: $46.99

Power supply: $39.99

Memory: $35.99

Storage: $37.99

Once I had my list of components, we went out to the warehouse to look at cases and peripherals.

Eli had never been to a junkyard before we started hanging out. But I've been going to junkyards my whole life with my dad and Uncle Gregor, because it's not like you can buy a brand-new seat for the 1965 Mustang you're working on. Nope. If the seat breaks, either you tell the customer it can't be fixed and they should get rid of it or you talk to the junkyard people until a good one comes along.

Mei's junkyard has a scrapyard of stuff that can get rained on, like cars for parts and tires for tire swings and old bathtubs for your goats to drink out of. Then there's the warehouse, full of chrome stuff and expensive stuff and some computer stuff too.

Inside the warehouse, there's a row of display counters across one end, with things that are old and cool but not valuable. This week, Mei had replaced a couple of huge ancient cell phones with a handheld game about jumping over barrels.

When I was younger, right after Mom and Dad let me see *Men in Black* for the first time, I thought maybe Mei had a bunch of alien technology hidden in the secret storage area behind the counters. I asked her about it once. She looked at me for a moment, like she was trying to decide whether she could trust me. Then she said, "Tell you what: you get an A in your tech class, and I'll show you what's in there." Probably she was just teasing me.

Probably. But I can take tech next year, and I'm going to work hard and get an A.

Just in case.

I guess some people might be disappointed to think about buying a bunch of dusty old stuff with their pile of money that they worked really hard for, but not me. Me? I see the possibilities. Those people who buy all new things . . . Well, in a couple of years, those same things end up right here in Mei's warehouse. And if they weren't junk to start out with, why would they be junk now? (Unless they break. Then they were probably junk to start out with.)

So, yeah, I like knowing I could turn that stuff into something amazing if I wanted to, something everyone would be impressed by, instead of treating it like trash.

"Keyboards are only three dollars!" Eli said, point-

ing. "And mice are only a dollar! You could buy five of them!"

"Yeah, but what would I do with five mice?" I said.

Eli stared at the cases in the thirty-dollar section, which were modded out with LEDs and stuff. All those lights look cool, but they don't actually add anything to how your computer works. A ten-dollar case works fine too.

Case: $10.00

Monitor: $25.00

Keyboard: $3.00

Mouse: $1.00

I took one last look around the warehouse and grinned. "That's everything. Let's go see what Mr. Z. thinks."

Mr. Z. and Oma were hanging out in the kitchen when we got home. Oma and her apron were hovering over a cake.

She beamed when she saw us. "Who would like a piece of Mohngugelhupf?"

When we said we would, she cut it with a fancy knife I'd found in Uncle Gregor's basement, and put the slices on Mom's special plates.

Honestly, it tasted pretty much like any other poppy-seed cake. Eli looked at me, and opened his mouth—but I got there first. "It's delicious, Oma. Like magic—cake magic."

Eli looked pretty surprised, but I don't think Oma noticed. She was too busy smiling.

Mr. Z. smiled at me and set his fork down. "Mrs. Schenk, I have not eaten such a delicious Mohngugel-hupf since I was a boy. Thank you for letting me assist you."

Oma did a little curtsy. *It was my pleasure,* she wrote.

I gave Eli a look.

"Nice work, Mrs. S.!" he said. "Maybe sometime we could try it with frosting, for an experiment. . . ." He studied his cake. "How did you get the fancy swirls in it?"

"First you make two batters," Oma said. "The ground poppy seeds go in one. Then you pour them both into the pan. Then you swirl them together, like this. . . ." She mimicked swirling her finger around in the pan.

"You stuck your hand in it?" I asked. "Please tell me you washed your hands first, Oma! What if you have ghostly germs?"

"Can you even wash your hands?" Eli said. "We never thought to check that! Here, let me design an experiment. . . ."

"I used a knife," Oma said, with dignity.

Mr. Z. cleared his throat. "Er, HD, shall we look at the list you have made?"

The rest of that week went pretty well. I sorted lots more boxes, and Eli practiced his routine in his new costume. It took him a while to get used to the eye-holes. We went to the library again too. We checked out some Spider-Man and Ms. Marvel and Moon Girl comics, and a Black Panther novel. Harry found me an article reviewing some free games I might want to try, once I build my computer. He found a book for Eli too, about a kid who tries out for a musical. And when we told him about the GOAT Obstacle Course, he said he might want to interview us about it for a future makerspace blog post, if that was okay with us.

We said that would probably be fine.

Then we ran back to Uncle Gregor's to figure out even more cool stuff to build for it.

Finally, on Friday afternoon, I opened the last box in Uncle Gregor's basement, and sorted it out. I put the wooden spools of thread into the "somebody else could use these" pile, because I already had thread for maker stuff. I put the issues of *Popular Mechanics* in the pile of stuff we could use, because Mr. Z. said sometimes they have cool projects. I put the wreath that was part wire and part really old dead plants and part dust into the trash, because the wire was all rusty. And I set the small glass bowl that wasn't chipped at all aside to ask Oma about, because some-times she really likes dishes, and it's hard to know which ones.

Then I called Dad up and told him he might want to come by for a minute, because I had something to show him.

"Not another ghost?" he asked.

"Nope," I told him. "Something even better. In fact, you might want to bring that envelope you've been saving."

Dad laughed, and promised he would.

Eli said this was a big event, the grand finale of my project, so we should put on a good show. We tidied up all the bags and boxes in their piles, and I tried to vacuum the basement floor, but a light started blink-ing on Uncle Gregor's shop vac, and we didn't know what to do about that.

Dad said that was fine, though—he'd take care of it before Uncle Gregor came back. He looked at all the piles of stuff for a long time, but he didn't move a single thing to a different pile. Then he came over and gave me a big hug and told me I did great, and that Uncle Gregor was going to be really impressed.

"I bet he'll love having all this space in his base-ment," Eli said, shuffling off to Buffalo in his sky-scraper costume. He'd been practicing, so this time the box only slipped around on his head and tilted a little bit, and he didn't crash into anything.

Dad and I applauded, and Eli took as much of a bow as he could manage in a cardboard box.

"Maybe Uncle Gregor will start a pinball arcade," I said. "Dad, there's this pinball machine I saw at the junkyard, and I bet it doesn't even need that much work—"

"You're going to have to talk to your uncle about that," Dad said, laughing. He looked at me. "Shall we do the honors now? Or after dinner, so your mom can say what she wants to say too?"

I scuffed my sneaker on the basement floor and smiled. "Tonight would be fine."

Eli and I walked the goats back to my house, and I told Oma about how I'd sorted all the boxes in the basement where she used to hang out, and how much space there'd be after we filled up Uncle Gregor's trash and recycling a few more times, and donated everything else. Then I tried to explain what a pinball machine was, but she said she knew what pinball was, we should see her moves, because she was a real plungeroo. That made Eli snort-laugh so hard he couldn't breathe. Then Dad came home and explained how it was legal for kids to play pinball now, and we say *pinball wizard*, not *plungeroo*. (She got a ghostly glint in her eye, so I think Uncle Gregor is going to have to get that pinball machine.)

After dinner, Dad stood up and tapped his glass with his fork. "Now, then." He cleared his throat. "HD, on behalf of your uncle, your mom, and myself, thank you for taking on such a big project for us, and for your commitment to seeing it through."

"Even when really unexpected stuff happened!" Eli said.

Dad nodded. "You've earned this. Great job, buddy." He gave me the envelope with the money that Uncle Gregor had left for me.

"Nice work, sweetie. We're so proud of you," Mom said. Then she smiled, and asked what I was going to do with all that money.

I rolled my eyes. I knew exactly what I was going to do with it, and so did everyone else. Eli and I had big plans for Rose's RadioJunkYardBirds the next day. (I told Dad he could drive us there. He seemed pleased about that.)

Finally, finally, FINALLY, it was time to buy my components.

18

But the next morning, Oma decided she needed me to take the lid off her crock, even though she has been doing the strength training course that Eli and I designed for her, so we knew she was strong enough to lift it herself.

"Mrs. S. sniffs the sauerkraut," Eli announced. "We don't know why she can smell things but not taste them. . . . Will it be ready? The crowd waits in silence. . . . What's this? She's asking HD to take the little plates out of the top of the crock. We've never seen this before! HD is pushing back, he's saying there's some stuff floating on the top and he's not sure it's a good idea to stick his hand in there. (Is it moldy, HD?)

HD reports it's not exactly moldy, he doesn't think, just kind of weird-looking. Ah, he's got some bacon tongs now, and he's picking up a plate with the tongs, and lifting it out. . . . (Careful, HD! If you break that, your mom's going to be mad.) The first plate is safely in the sink! Now for the next one. . . . Whoops! Good catch, Mrs. S.!"

Oma examined the sauerkraut. She floated closer and sniffed it again.

I sniffed too. It didn't smell like old socks anymore— it smelled kind of like a pickle.

Oma looked up at me, and beamed. "We must call Mr. Ziedrich!"

"Okay, we can call him as soon as we get back from Rose's," I told her.

"No, no—we must call him right now!" Oma insisted.

I shrugged. "You can email him yourself and see if he can come help you while we're gone, if you want."

"No!" Oma said. "You must stay and help me!"

I took a deep breath, like Mom does when Asad throws a fit. Sometimes Oma wasn't all that different.

"Here's the thing, Mrs. S.," Eli explained. "This morning, we've got to do HD's plan, because we've already worked it out with his dad, and he's been waiting to do this all year. But after that, we can help you. So, what is your plan, aside from calling Mr. Z., and us helping you? What kind of grand finale do you need for your sauerkraut?"

Oma blinked. "Well . . ."

But I was thinking now. "Oma, sauerkraut isn't exactly a breakfast food anyway, is it? So really, we should try it tonight instead. What if we had a sauerkraut-tasting party, with sausages and stuff?"

"Yes!" Eli said, pumping his fist. "I'll be your announcer, and you can make some brownies or something."

"We could invite Mr. Z., and maybe Ms. Stevermer," I said. Oma hadn't interrupted yet, so I kept going. "You want everyone to taste it, don't you?"

"Will that work for you?" Eli asked. "Because we should probably tell HD's mom before she goes to the store, if we want that to happen."

Oma still didn't look that happy about it, but finally, she nodded. "I suppose it will do."

So Dad drove me and Eli to Rose's RadioJunkYard-Birds. One thing I like about my dad is that he knows how to stay out of the way and let a person do their thing. We told him we were cool, so he went off to look at speakers and let Mei know about some left-over parts from the auto body shop, in case she wanted to buy them, and to see if she had the right kind of Harley-Davidson wheel hub in stock. Dad knows some stuff about electronics, but mostly about car electronics. (Well, and tanks, and stuff like that—that's what he worked on in the army.)

First we went to see Grace.

I have never had more than a hundred dollars in my life before. All those twenty-dollar bills barely fit in my wallet! When we went in, I looked around at everything I could buy, and I had to grin. If I was just some normal kid, I could have bought a fancy game system and gone right home and played it.

But that's not me. I had a plan.

"Hey, HD. Hey, Eli. You want to see something?" Grace nodded at us.

I was trying to play it cool, like I did this all the time, but I couldn't stop grinning. "Hey, Grace. I think I'm ready to do some buying today."

Grace's eyebrows went up, and she gave me the nod, real slow, impressed. "So you got the job done. Nice work, HD."

"Let's start with the CPU we talked about, and work down the list," I told her. "Eli, will you keep track of the project costs?"

Grace handed Eli a calculator. He turned it on and got ready.

It was pretty awesome, to be able to point to something and just be, like, "Yeah, let's go with that one," and watch Grace pile it all up into a stack for me to buy. At least, it was awesome until I found out somebody else had already bought the motherboard I wanted.

"I'm sorry," Grace told me. "I was hoping we might get more in before you needed yours. This would work fine too, though." She handed me another option. "It's a little bit newer, it would work with your CPU and the rest of your components, and it's getting great reviews. It's twenty dollars more, though."

I bit my lip. My project budget was already tight. "Eli, what would the total be if I bought that motherboard?"

Eli did some more calculating. "It's $280.95 so far."

"You brought your student ID card, though, right?" Grace asked.

I nodded. "Can you subtract five percent for my student discount?"

Eli multiplied my total by 0.95, because 100% minus 5% is 95%. "With your student discount, it's $266.90."

"Can I use a plastic-bag coupon too?" I asked Grace. (Everyone in town brings their extra bags in to Rose's, because you get a 5%-off coupon. That way,

Rose doesn't ever have to buy from the plastic bag salesman who makes her mad, and people don't have to worry so much about their plastic bags clogging up the ocean.)

"Sure," Grace said. So I gave her the plastic bags we'd brought, and she gave me my 5%-off coupon.

Eli subtracted another 5%. "It's only $253.56 now!"

"Oh yeah," I said, and grinned.

"Don't forget, I have to charge you sales tax too," Grace reminded us. "That's ten percent these days."

Eli multiplied my $253.56 by 1.1, to add the 10%. "Oh, man—we're up to $278.92 now!"

I sighed. "And I don't have a case, or a monitor, or a keyboard, or a mouse yet."

"Well, you can find a case and do your computer build, and add your peripherals later," Grace reminded me.

"Yeah, I know," I said.

"You might want to check the warehouse before you make any final decisions anyway," Grace said. "Mei got some good-looking stuff in this week."

"Thanks," I told her. "Let's go take a look, Eli."

Grace smiled. "I'll hold these for now. Bring the calculator back when you're done."

We passed Mei in the scrapyard, where she was unbolting a side mirror from a 1963 Impala for somebody, and she nodded at us and kept working. Dad says Mei doesn't really do small talk.

Grace was right—there was some good stuff in the warehouse. I checked a monitor to make sure the display looked pretty good, and I asked Eli to test all the keys on the keyboard that looked the cleanest, to make sure none of them stuck or anything, while I untangled and tested a mouse.

When I had a good one, I brought it over to Eli, who finished up his keyboard and nodded. "This one's fine," he said. "I mean, it's pretty dirty, but it works okay."

"Good work," I told Eli, and he did a tap move, and bowed. "What's my total so far?"

Eli checked his notes, and punched some more numbers into the calculator. "With the monitor, the mouse, and the keyboard, we're at $307.70, including discounts and sales tax."

I sighed. "I had to buy Oma's glue, so I've only got $296.06. I need a case to start the build, so I guess I'll have to wait on the monitor for now."

Eli shifted his weight from one foot to the other. "I have some money too."

I shook my head. I had to do this myself. "Thanks, but nah." I walked over to the cases, leaving the monitor I'd picked behind.

There was a plain black case that I didn't remember seeing before. I lifted it off of the top shelf and turned it around. You can't just pick a case based on what it looks like from the front. You have to check it out to make sure it doesn't have any broken parts or anything.

And this case? This one had a surprise for me.

"What's that?" Eli asked, pointing inside.

"Someone left the motherboard in this case," I told him. It looked good too.

"Will you go find Mei?" I asked, picking up the case and holding it tight. "Tell her I have a question."

Eli nodded, and ran.

If I bought this case and the peripherals, I wouldn't have enough left for the motherboard Grace was holding for me. Maybe it would be better to get a motherboard I knew worked, and wait for the rest.

But if this motherboard did work, I'd get a case and a motherboard for a really good deal, and I might even have enough left over for a game or something. Plus, I'd have a cool story about how I found it.

Eli came back with Mei. Mei folded her arms and waited.

I nodded at Mei. "Thanks for coming to take a look," I said. "Seems there's a motherboard in this case. Is it still ten dollars?"

Mei looked at the case. She looked at the handwritten sign that said ALL CASES IN THIS SECTION $10. NO EXCEPTIONS. She said, "Yep."

"You know anything about it?" I asked.

"Guy brought it in like that a couple days ago with a bunch of other stuff," Mei told me. "It all looked brand-new."

Yeah, that's what I thought when I saw it too—no dust or anything. "Is it okay if I take it in to see what Grace thinks about the motherboard?"

Mei nodded. "I'll get you a flatbed cart for all this. You know all sales are final, so make sure you really want it before you buy it."

I nodded. Buying stuff at a junkyard is a commitment.

Eli and I wheeled the cart back to the electronics department, me pushing and Eli pointing out potholes and making sure nothing fell off.

We waited until Grace was done helping Mrs. Alvarez set up her new laptop. After Mrs. Alvarez thanked Grace a few more times and finally left, we brought the cart up to the counter.

"Mrs. Alvarez makes really, really good brownies," Eli told Grace.

Grace grinned. "Well, then, if she brings me more than I can handle, I know who to call. Now, what have you two found?"

I lifted up the case and set it on the counter. "Mei said we could bring it in to show you. What do you think?"

Grace peered inside. She took a screwdriver from a big mug on the counter, removed the screws from the back of the case, lining them up carefully on the counter, and slid off one of the sides. She tipped the case over so we could look down at the motherboard.

Eli's mouth was practically hanging open as he watched her work. But I didn't tease him, because I was pretty interested too. I mean, it's not like I'd seen anyone actually do anything like this in real life before, even though Mr. Z. had told me all about how it works, and Harry had found me some videos and photos of people doing their builds.

Carefully she unscrewed the motherboard from the tray, lining those screws up in a different row on the counter. She lifted it out by the edges and turned it over. "Looks brand-new. Is this from that batch Mei just bought?"

"Yeah, that's what she said," I told Grace.

"That guy said he was testing out equipment for a magazine," Grace said. "Personally, I wouldn't buy a beat-up board, but I considered some of his stuff myself." She handed me the motherboard. "You want to make sure none of the pins are bent, and that the capacitors aren't damaged. If they look good, you've got a decent chance that it'll work. Unless it's fried, of course."

So I held up the motherboard and checked out the pins and the capacitors. "They look good to me." I handed it back to her.

Grace nodded. "Could be worth a try. You know it fits in the case you picked, and it's got a good layout. Plenty of slots for your memory, if you want to add more later. And it's a nice-looking case too—very classic." She picked up the box for the CPU I'd chosen and read the compatibility notes. "This CPU should work fine with that board."

Eli put the calculator down on the counter. "Can I have a piece of paper?"

Grace handed him the back of a flyer and a big flat contractor's pencil.

Eli folded the flyer in half the long way and started checking the prices on the components again and carefully writing out two lists, one if I bought the case, one if I didn't.

Grace handed Eli another flyer. "Better make a third list too: what you're going to need if HD gets this home and it doesn't work."

Eli nodded solemnly, writing the numbers down and double-checking them.

I didn't like changing my plan at this stage, but I didn't really have a choice, unless I wanted to wait until they got my original motherboard back in stock. If I did that, I'd probably miss the fair. "What do you think?" I asked Grace. "Should I buy it?"

Grace shrugged. "It depends. You know the risks

of buying used equipment: You can't return it, and it might not work. If you want to play it safe, you go with a new motherboard. But then it might take you longer to buy all your peripherals and get to try out your computer."

Eli looked up from his lists. "If you go with the motherboard in the case, you can buy everything today, and you'd have $44.93 left over. If you get the new motherboard instead, you're going to have to earn $21.57 more for your monitor."

He passed the lists to me, and I read through them. Then I took a deep breath. Sometimes you just have to try stuff. And if it doesn't work out, you try again. "I'll take the case and the monitor, and skip the other motherboard," I said.

"Woo-hoo!" Eli shouted.

Grace smiled at me, and started ringing up the whole pile.

I got out my wallet, showed her my student ID, gave her my coupon, and counted out more money than I ever had in my life.

Grace gave me my change, and helped me screw the motherboard back in and put the case together again. "If I were you, I'd stop by the library and ask them to print out the manual for that motherboard," she told me, writing the manufacturer and model number down.

I nodded. Mr. Z. always likes to check the manuals. "We'll do that," I told her. "Thanks for the help."

"Anytime," Grace said. "Let me know how it goes."

"We should fill out the customer service survey for Grace, since she did such a good job," Eli said as we pushed the cart around to find Dad.

I agreed. I never would have done that for Dennis, who used to work there.

Eli was grinning a huge grin, so I guess he was feeling like things had gone pretty well.

I guess I probably was too.

19

That evening, Mr. Z. and Ms. Stevermer came over for the sauerkraut party. I showed Eli how to make strawberry lemonade like Grandmom Davis taught me. Mom and Asad had a fight about whether or not Asad was going to get any dessert if he didn't at least try Ms. Stevermer's coleslaw. Mr. Z. brought his favorite kind of potato salad, and I told him all about our trip to Rose's, and the motherboard I found, and how Grace helped me check it out. He thought it sounded good too. And Dad and Oma barbecued sausages. We found out that she doesn't get burned even when she sticks her hand through the barbecue grill to move the coals around. So, that was educational.

When all the sausages were barbecued and ready, Oma floated a bowl of sauerkraut over and set it down in front of Mr. Z. *"Guten Appetit!"* she wrote, and held it up for everyone.

Mr. Z. nodded at the sign. He took a forkful of sauerkraut and put it in his mouth. We all held our breath while he chewed.

He swallowed, and smiled. "It reminds me of my mother's, only better. There's something a little bit different about it. . . ."

I opened my mouth to tell him about the juniper berries, but Oma elbowed me and wrote, *"That is all thanks to my secret ingredient."*

Mr. Z. chuckled. "Ah, yes, every cook has her secrets. My mother's was caraway."

Oma smiled, and finally let the rest of us try some too.

I took the first bite. It was pretty weird, but not that bad.

"It's like pickle salad," Eli said, putting his fork down.

Dad laughed. "Or pickle coleslaw, maybe. But you should really eat it on a sausage." He handed us our sausages, and showed us how to put spicy brown mustard on one side of the bun and sauerkraut on the other, and then squish the whole thing down so you could take a bite.

"Kind of like a sausage with pickle salad on it," I said, grinning at Eli over mine.

"This is the best sauerkraut I've ever had," Dad said. "Nice work, Oma!"

Oma wrote that of course it was. It was her specialty, after all, and she'd been making it longer than he'd been alive.

Asad wouldn't try it. But he did draw a picture of Oma in her pj's and a cape, defeating some kind of giant octopus robot by throwing sauerkraut at it. (At least, that's what he said it was.) After dinner, Oma brought out her special pan. When she flipped it over, her mohn gugelhupf came out perfectly—but Asad took one look at it and started to cry. "I want brownies!"

Eli looked at Asad, and at the frowning ghost, then at me. "Maybe we should go finish getting ready for your computer build."

I nodded. "Yeah. Let's go do that."

Mom offered to help Oma can her sauerkraut the next day. Oma wanted us to help, but Mom said she didn't think two almost-teenage boys, an unpredictable ghost, a bunch of glass jars, and a huge pot of boiling water were a good combination, so Dad and Asad gave me and Eli a ride to Maple Falls.

We stopped at the library on our way. Dad and Asad stayed in the car while Eli and I went inside.

"Hey, HD. Hey, Eli," Harry said, giving us the nod. "Got any interesting questions for me?"

I nodded back. "Can you find me the manual for this motherboard?" I passed him the information.

"You mean, this is the big day?" Harry asked. "Or are you refining your plan?"

"This is it," I told him. "I got my components and my peripherals, and we're on our way to build my computer."

Harry got up and came around from behind his desk. He reached out his hand, and we did one of his cool Harry special handshakes—the kind he usually only does when you finish your summer-reading-program goals or win the Battle of the Books.

When I told him how much Eli helped with all the calculations and everything, he did one with Eli too.

"I am very impressed," he said, going back to his chair. "Very impressed indeed, and happy to do my part for this endeavor. Now, let me see . . . Aha!" Harry tapped some more keys, and the printer whirred out some paper. "Anything else?" he asked, handing it to me.

"Yeah, one more thing," I said. "Could we get some entry forms for the county fair?"

"Sure thing," he said, turning back to his keyboard. "You're entering your computer, so the technology category. . . . What about you, Eli?"

"I've got a tap recital, but I don't need a form for that," Eli said. "Ms. Izdebski takes care of it for our class. We need a form for sauerkraut, though."

Harry nodded. "Sauerkraut—so, in the jams and pickles category, right?"

"Yeah, I think so," I told him.

"Looks like entry forms are due a week before the fair opens, along with the entry fee, so you want to get those in soon. Then you check in at the Entry Registration Booth by nine a.m. on the date your category is judged." He clicked a few more clicks, and the printer whirred again.

"Here's the instructions too." He handed over the sheets, and Eli started reading them. Harry smiled at me. "You know, I've never entered the fair, but I make a mean coconut shortbread. Let me know how it goes for you, and maybe I'll think about it next year."

"Why don't you just enter it?" I asked. "I mean, I hear Mrs. Alvarez's cookies are pretty tough to beat, but maybe she'll make a pie or something instead. What have you got to lose by trying?"

Harry looked at me—really looked at me, not like *Yeah, whatever, kid.* "You know, HD, I think that's some very good advice. I just might do that."

When Dad and Asad dropped me and Eli and all my computer stuff off at Maple Falls, Mr. Z. was waiting for us in the project room. Someday I'm going to have a project room in my house. It has two big tables that fold up if you need to get them out of the way, and a bunch of folding chairs, and pretty good lighting too.

"We brought everything, Mr. Z.!" Eli said.

"Including the manual for that motherboard," I told Mr. Z.

"Excellent," Mr. Z. said. He isn't exactly a pump-your-fist kind of guy, but even he was grinning today. He cleared his throat. "HD, I have something for you—something that might help with this project." He handed me a small black case.

I took it from him, and slowly unzipped it. It was a set of screwdrivers, all lined up in their pockets: slots, Phillips, and stars, two different sizes each, with an anti-static wrist strap tucked in too.

"This is my old computer tool kit," Mr. Z. told me. "Now that you are building computers, I thought that you might like to have it."

It was perfect. But my eyes felt funny, and my chest kind of hurt, like I couldn't breathe. How was Mr. Z. going to make anything without his tools? "But—you might need it."

Mr. Z. shook his head. "I don't think I will need it anytime soon, and I would be happy knowing you're putting it to good use."

"Let me know if you ever want to borrow it back, though, okay?" I told him. "You can, anytime you want to build something."

"I will," he said, smiling. "I promise."

"*Danke*, Mr. Z.," I told him. "*Danke* very much."

"*Gern geschehen*, HD." Mr. Z. turned to the project tables. "Now line everything up, and we will take a look."

So Eli and I lined everything up in the middle of one of the project tables while Mr. Z. moved slowly down the line, examining each part. He was using his cane today. When he got to the end, he nodded. "Now you are ready to build something beautiful."

I took a deep breath and started ripping the plastic wrap off of everything. It was pretty much like Christmas, even if I did already know what everything was. Eli put all the packaging in the trash can for me, and Mr. Z. checked the manuals. I opened my project notebook, and turned to my list of steps.

HD'S COMPUTER BUILD:

Put on the anti-static wristband. Attach the clip to a metal area on the computer case.

Unscrew the case screws and slide off the sides.

Install the I/O shield into the case. (Already in there!)

Remove the motherboard from the case.

Install the CPU in the socket on the motherboard.

Attach the CPU fan on top of the CPU.

Push the memory down into the slot on the motherboard.

Install the power supply in the case.

Attach the motherboard to the case.

Connect the CPU fan, the case fan, the power supply, the speaker, and the power button to the motherboard.

Unclip your wristband.

Connect the power cord to the power supply.

Connect the monitor to the computer.

Plug the computer and monitor into the electrical outlets.

Power everything on to see if it lights up.

Unplug everything from the electrical outlets.

Clip your wristband again.

Install the solid-state drive.

Connect everything else to the motherboard.

Manage your cables.

Put the sides back on the case, and screw them in.

Unclip your wristband again.

Connect the keyboard and mouse.

Plug the computer and monitor back into the electrical outlets.

Power it all up.

Have fun with your BRAND-NEW COMPUTER!!!

First I got the anti-static wristband out of Mr. Z.'s tool kit, and I put it on. Mr. Z. helped me fasten it, and I figured out where I could clip it to one of the metal parts of the case. Even a tiny, tiny bit of static electricity can fry your delicate computer components, way smaller than you could feel. But this way, it would go into the case, instead of the components. (Besides, it looks pretty cool and maker-like.)

I let Eli blow the dust out of the keyboard with Mr. Z.'s can of compressed air, because he was a big help, with all that calculating. Besides, I've used the compressed air lots of times.

"It's still kind of dirty," Eli said.

So Mr. Z. got a bottle of rubbing alcohol, some cotton swabs, and an old toothbrush out of his supplies box. I said it was fine if Eli cleaned up the keyboard and the mouse while I worked on my computer build, if he wanted to. Eli said sure, he'd never brushed anything but teeth with a toothbrush before, but he'd give it a try.

Then he gave me the can, and, very carefully, I used the compressed air on the motherboard, in case there was any microscopic dust on there. It still looked fine to me. But it wasn't like I'd seen a lot of motherboards in real life, out of their packages.

I got out the largest Phillips screwdriver from Mr.

Z.'s tool kit, and I unscrewed all the screws on the back of the case. Then I lifted one side off, just like Grace had. Then the other. I checked that step off the list.

Then I unscrewed all the screws holding the motherboard in place, and lined them up on the table.

"You can set it down on this, to protect it while you work on it," Mr. Z. said, handing me a square of black foam, just like the one that comes with brand-new motherboards in the computer-build videos I'd watched.

"Thanks," I told him, setting the foam next to the screws. Carefully I lifted the motherboard up by the edges, not touching all those delicate circuits, and put it down on the foam.

For the CPU, I turned to the diagrams Harry had found for me. One of them matched my CPU socket exactly, so that's what I followed. I lifted the little wire arm all the way up, out of the way. Then I held my breath; carefully, carefully, carefully lifted up the CPU by the edges; lined up the triangle on the corner with the mark on the socket, and lowered it down. I gave it just a little push, to make sure it was settled right. Then I lowered the little wire arm again, and it sucked the CPU into the socket and locked it in.

Mr. Z. gave me a high five after that one, even

though that's not usually his thing. CPUs are expensive, so if you mess that part up, well . . . let's just say he knew I was nervous about it.

The fan that came with the CPU already had special paste on it, and it came with screws too. So all I had to do was align the underside of the fan with the CPU, like it showed in the diagram, then stick it on and screw it down. I know how to assemble things carefully, and obviously I know how to use a screwdriver.

The memory was trickier. It had a little clip thing on one side of the motherboard slot that I had to unlatch and open. Then I had to match up the notch on the memory stick to the bump in the slot, to put it in the right way. I had to push the stick down into the side of the slot without the clip, and then the other side. The edge of the stick is really narrow, and if you bend it, the whole thing's ruined, so I was nervous. It took me a few tries to push it down hard enough to snap it in so that the clip would close again. I had to take a deep breath and shake out my hands after that. But Mr. Z. said I did great.

The first time I tried to put the power supply into the case, I put it in upside down. But it was pretty obvious that wasn't going to work, since the screw holes on the power supply didn't align with the holes on the

case. So I took it out, turned it around, and tried again, without Mr. Z. having to say anything about it. That way worked just fine. I tucked that big octopus nest of cables out of the way so I could see what I was doing.

I knew how to install the motherboard, because I'd just taken it out of the case. My case already had the little brass standoffs screwed into the side of the case wall, so all I had to do was match up the screw holes on the motherboard with those brass standoffs and screw it in again.

I didn't have a diagram or anything for the next part, because every motherboard and every power supply and every case is a little bit different. Instead, I read the tiny, tiny writing near the pins and plugs on the motherboard, and matched it up to the tiny, tiny writing on the cables. Then I had to turn the connectors around, or sometimes pick from two connectors on the same cable, and see which one had the round and square combination that matched the socket, kind of like a puzzle. There were a couple of mysterious parts I had to ask Mr. Z. about—like, who knew that "ATX12V1" matched "pwr"? But he said that's what he was there for, and I was doing great.

I connected the power cord. That was easy. And I already knew how to connect the monitor, and how to unclip my wristband, and plug everything in for the first test.

Mr. Z. grinned. "Ready?"

Eli came over so he could see too.

I grinned, reached out, and pushed the power buttons on the computer and the monitor.

The monitor's power light came on. But not my computer. No case fan, no CPU fan, no beeps, no lights. Nothing.

"Why isn't it doing anything?" Eli asked me.

It took me a minute to make the words come out past the lump in my throat. "I guess it's fried."

"No, we cannot say that yet," Mr. Z. said. "First you must double-check everything you've done so far."

"You mean, maybe it was fine until I broke it?" I asked. That really didn't make me feel any better.

"No, I meant that it may not be broken," Mr. Z. said. "A connection might not be pushed in far enough, or a plug might not be seated correctly."

"Okay," I said, even though I didn't think this was going to help at all.

Mr. Z. looked at my face. "But first, I think we will have a snack break. Troubleshooting on an empty stomach is not very effective."

20

I didn't think I was going to be able to eat anything. Not with my computer all busted like that. But Mr. Z. said he needed some more coffee to get his brain going, so after I unplugged everything again, we went down to the Maple Falls cafeteria for a snack.

Mr. Z. got his coffee, and Gladys decided Eli and I needed to try her special cinnamon rolls. They were almost as big as our heads. Since she was watching us, I took a bite, just to be polite. It was pretty good. Somehow I ended up eating the whole thing while Mr. Z. and I went over the list of steps, what I'd done so far, how to double-check them, and what it would look like if something was busted.

After that, we washed our hands again and dried them off really well, and went back to the project room to try again.

First I sniffed the case. Nothing smelled like smoke or electricity gone wrong. Mr. Z. said that was a very good sign that I hadn't fried anything.

Then I started from the beginning of my instructions, double-checking each step. I pushed down gently on the CPU fan, and the memory card, and everywhere the power supply was connected.

Meanwhile, Mr. Z. walked around the table, checking my work from all angles. Suddenly he stopped, and smiled. "HD, I think I see the problem. Come, stand right here, and tell me what you observe."

I went around the table to where he was standing, looking at the back of my case. "I see all the ports that the keyboard and stuff plug into, only they're not plugged in right now. I can kind of see the case fan through the air holes, but it isn't moving. I see the power cord plugged into the power supply—oh!" I grinned at Mr. Z. "And the power switch on the power supply is in the 'off' position!"

So I plugged everything back in again, and switched on the power supply.

And this time—it lit up! The fans whirred to life, and the computer beeped!

"It's alive!" Eli yelled, pretending to be Dr. Frankenstein.

"It sure is," I said. "But we're not done yet, Eli."

So Eli got back to work cleaning up the keyboard and the mouse, and I went back to my checklist.

Time to power it back down and unplug everything, and to clip my wristband on again so I could install my solid-state drive. I lined it up in the bracket and screwed the sides into the case. Then I had to check the tiny, tiny writing so I could get it hooked up to a data port on the motherboard, and then to the power supply.

Then . . . more tiny, tiny writing, and more connectors! It was time to hook everything else up too—the LED indicators on the case, the USB port, all of that stuff. Mr. Z. said that even back when his eyes were better, that part took him the longest.

Next was the part Mr. Z. said took him the second longest: cable management. All that stuff I had to hook up had cables running all over the place, and you can't just leave them lying around where they might get in the way of the fans. Besides, it looks like a rat's nest, and that's no good. So I used some cable ties and some plastic twist ties to get everything organized.

I unclipped my wristband and checked out the

keyboard and mouse that Eli had cleaned up for me. They looked really good—almost brand-new. "Nice," I told him. "Thanks, man." I hooked them up, then put the sides back on the case and screwed them in.

Now there were check marks next to every single step, except for two.

Power it all up.

Have fun with your BRAND-NEW COMPUTER!!!

I couldn't stop smiling. It was sitting right there, just like I'd imagined: my own computer.

"Go ahead and plug it in," Mr. Z. told me.

So I unclipped my anti-static wrist strap, took a deep breath, and plugged in the computer I built. And then I came around, and I pushed the power button on the computer and on the monitor.

The indicator lights came on. I held my breath.

The computer made a little noise, and then another . . . And then words appeared on my computer monitor! The BIOS screen appeared, exactly like it was supposed to! Everything worked!

Eli and I pumped our fists and jumped around for a minute while Mr. Z. pressed the intercom and asked Gladys to bring us some ginger ale in fancy plastic glasses so we could have a toast. Then he walked down the halls inviting everyone around to come see what we built. He introduced us as his friends HD,

the maker, and Eli, the scientist. I tried to play it cool, kind of. But everyone was so impressed that I had built a whole computer from parts I bought myself that I couldn't help but grin.

"Imagine what it's going to be like at the fair!" Eli said happily.

I pictured myself in front of everyone I knew, explaining they could build one too, as long as they were careful and double-checked everything, and wore an anti-static wrist strap so they didn't accidentally electrocute their components. Harry would give me the nod, and maybe do another special handshake, and Grace and Rose and Mei would cheer, and Ms. Stevermer might make a note in her notebook, and my parents would be prouder than they'd ever been. And I was pretty sure that by the time I walked into middle school next year, everyone was going to know who I was, and what I could do.

I smiled.

When Dad came to pick us and the computer up, he said we were going straight to Frank's Diner to celebrate. Mr. Z. had a pool tournament, though, and couldn't join us.

"Thanks, Mr. Z.," I told him. "This was pretty much the best project ever."

"Oh, I am sure the next one you dream up will be twice as exciting," Mr. Z. said, smiling. "And I will be twice as happy to help."

At the diner, Frank made me and Eli wear paper birthday crowns, even though it wasn't our birthdays, and took a picture of us with my computer on the table. "For the wall," he said, nodding seriously.

Frank's wall is covered in photos of everyone who comes to the diner: Little League teams in uniform waving hot dogs, and the girls' karate team pretending to chop the diner tables in half with their hands, and the cast of *The Music Man* hovering around the biggest ice cream cake Frank ever made, still in their costumes. Not to mention photos to show that Frank's two-foot-long sub sandwich is longer than a new baby, and people pretending to feed burgers to their prize-winning giant cabbages, and all that. I liked knowing my computer would be up there too.

After we finished the grilled cheese–BLT hybrid that I invented, and Eli's plain grilled cheese on sourdough, with mayonnaise instead of ketchup for his fries, Eli looked at me. "You know what sounds really good right now?"

I grinned. "A brownie."

Dad laughed, and got up to go talk to Frank. "Just don't let your oma hear you say that."

I was feeling good about things when we pulled into our garage and lugged everything inside. But as soon as we came in, before Mom could even tell me congratulations, the ghost said, "Hans Dieter, we have a problem." She floated over and dropped a piece of paper right into my hands.

"Marietta, please let HD in the door first," Mom said, sighing.

But Oma just kept floating right in front of my face.

I read it silently. I guess Mom and Oma had had a conversation while we were at the diner.

Oma: When will the Pickle Parade happen?

Mom: I don't believe I've ever heard of the Pickle Parade. There's the Veterans Day Parade—Hans Peter and I usually drive some of the older veterans in that.

Oma: Do you never attend the fair?

Mom: Of course we attend the fair. Hans Peter enters a car every year, and I enter vegetables I've grown. I've got a giant kohlrabi that's coming along really well this year, as long as we keep those goats away from it.

Oma: But you don't watch the winners drive through town in the Pickle Parade?

Mom: I'll need to check, but I don't think they do that anymore.

Oma: But how does the town honor the winners?

Mom: Well, they award a blue ribbon to the winning entries—I've got one for last year's giant cabbage, and Hans Peter won his three years ago for the restored Volkswagen Beetle.

Oma: But what about the Pickle Prize?

Mom: I'm not familiar with the Pickle Prize.

Oma: It's a golden trophy with a marble base, etched with the past winners of the pickling contest. The winner and her family ride through town in the mayor's car. The winner wears the Pickle Queen's corsage and her best hat, and carries the Pickle Prize.

Mom: I'm afraid I've never heard of that happening.

Oma: I must win the Pickle Prize.

Mom: Well, HD is doing everything he can to help you with that. But not everything is about winning, right?

Oma: I must win.

I sighed. Mom had already told her that things had changed, but she wasn't exactly taking it well. What was I supposed to do—tell the mayor she had to have a Pickle Parade and drive my great-great-grandma the ghost around if she won? And tell everyone they were supposed to wave back and cheer, even though they couldn't see her?

Mom walked right through the ghost and gave me a big hug. "Never mind that right now—this is your time to celebrate! Now show us what you built."

Mom doesn't love computers the way I do, but I appreciated her changing the subject. So I set up the computer and all the peripherals in the family room. The ghost fell silent as the computer booted up.

I'd done it a few times already, but I still held my breath as the computer beeped and hummed to life, and I still smiled when the BIOS screen came up.

But before I could explain what was going on, or how I put it all together, the ghost wanted to know where her sauerkraut application was for the fair.

"We got that too, Mrs. S.," Eli told her.

But it was hard to hear her answer, because Mom was explaining to Asad that no, we couldn't watch TV right now, we were right in the middle of something very important to his brother, and didn't he want to see what the computer did? And Asad was asking whether he could play *Minecraft* on my computer, so I had to tell him no, it wasn't really set up to play games, or anything yet, since I'd just built it this afternoon.

"Then what's it good for?" Asad asked.

I sighed, and turned the computer off again.

Mom tried to stop me, but then Asad knocked his water all over her, and Dad went for paper towels, and Eli was trying to answer Oma's questions about the Pickle Parade. They didn't even notice when I unplugged it all, put it back in the box, and took it downstairs to my room.

I put the box in the corner, and sat down on my bed. Mom and Dad must have let Asad watch his program, because he didn't come down to bug me, and Oma probably hadn't finished with Eli yet. Usually I love having time to myself to do maker stuff. But right then I didn't feel like making any notes for new project ideas. Yeah, sure, I still needed to figure out a plan for some software so my computer would do something. But I'd worked really hard on it, making my plan, earning all that money, doing my build. I just wanted to enjoy this part a little bit longer before I got back to work.

I stared up at my posters until they swam a little, and sniffed back my feelings. I bet Shuri's first computer ran half of Wakanda.

There was a tap at my door, and then Mom came in. When she saw my face, she came over and gave me a hug. "What's wrong, sweetie?"

I shrugged. "It's okay, Mom—you don't have to pretend to be all excited about my project."

She gave me a look. "Of course I'm excited about it! Just because you're growing up doesn't mean I have to stop being excited about everything you do."

I turned away. "It's not like it's that hard."

"Maybe not for you, but I've never built a computer," she said. "Honey, I'm sorry your brother and your grandma didn't respect your time tonight. But I'll tell you what: Why don't I find out if Asad can spend the day at the fair with his friend Liya when your presentation is scheduled, and we can celebrate your computer properly? We could invite Mr. Ziedrich, and Grace, and that librarian you're always talking about. . . ."

"I'm not always talking about Harry," I told her. "We just have some things in common."

She nodded. "Like computers, I bet. So, how does that sound?"

"Well, they might have their own stuff to do," I told her. "I told Harry he should enter his cookies this year, and Mr. Z. is bringing Rodgers and Hammerstein."

"But if they are available, is it something you would like to see happen?" Mom asked.

I didn't tell her that's pretty much how I always dreamed it would be, ever since I thought up this project. I just nodded.

But I think she guessed how I felt about it anyway.

21

The next day, Dad wanted to take a bunch of the stuff from the "somebody else could use this" pile to the junkyard before he had to take Asad to camp. I offered to come along and help, since it was my project, and since I love the junkyard, but Dad said my job was to stay home and keep Asad out of trouble for half an hour, since Asad isn't good at keeping his hands to himself at the junkyard.

"Can't Oma watch him?" I asked.

"Your mom and I would feel better if there's some-one around that other people can see and hear, just in case," Dad said. "I'll be five minutes away. Call me if you need anything."

I sighed. "I guess we have to get our entry forms done for the fair anyway."

HUCKLEBERRY COUNTY FAIR ENTRY FORM

Exhibitor's name: _HD Schenk_

Phone number: _(206) 888-1212_

All entries are to be brought to the Entry Registration Booth by 9 a.m. on the date that category will be judged.

Category: _Technology_

Description: _the computer I built from scratch_

Exhibitor category:

PEEWEE____

YOUTH___X____

IF YOUTH: GRADE IN SCHOOL JUST COMPLETED___6____

ADULT____

SENIOR CITIZEN____

Special accommodations needed: _electrical outlet for computer_

I understand that I must present my entry to the judges when scheduled in order to be eligible to win. NO EXCEPTIONS.

The owner of the exhibit releases the Huckleberry County Fair from liability from any loss, damage, or injury to livestock or any other property while such property is on the grounds of the Huckleberry County Fair.

Exhibitor's Signature_____HD Schenk_____

HUCKLEBERRY COUNTY FAIR ENTRY FORM

Exhibitor's name: _Mrs. Marietta Schenk_

Phone number: _(206) 888-1212_

All entries are to be brought to the Entry Registration Booth by 9 a.m. on the date that category will be judged.

Category: _Pickles & Jams_

Description: _my finest sauerkraut_

Exhibitor category:

PEEWEE____

YOUTH____

IF YOUTH: GRADE IN SCHOOL JUST COMPLETED____

ADULT____

SENIOR CITIZEN _X_

Special accommodations needed:_____

I understand that I must present my entry to the judges when scheduled in order to be eligible to win. NO EXCEPTIONS.

The owner of the exhibit releases the Huckleberry County Fair from liability from any loss, damage, or injury to livestock or any other property while such property is on the grounds of the Huckleberry County Fair.

Exhibitor's Signature_____ _Marietta Schenk_____

Oma handed me her entry form.

Eli read it over my shoulder. "What if the judges can't see her? Maybe she should request an accommodation."

"Oma, do you think you might need an accommodation, since you can't be seen and heard by people?" I asked.

Oma sniffed. "Why would I need an accommodation? There is nothing wrong with me."

Eli stiffened. "Sometimes people who are smart and work hard still need accommodations to do their best." He looked away. "I do, sometimes."

I watched him for a minute. He didn't look like he wanted to say any more right now. "Is it okay if I explain, Eli?" I asked.

He nodded, but he didn't look up. Eli likes to talk, but he doesn't like talking about this. He doesn't like people not understanding either. So I help him out, when he says it's okay.

"Look, Oma, we're not all built exactly the same, and sometimes people need accommodations. You've seen how careful Eli was when he wrote to you. That's because he was thinking hard about what he was saying, but it's also because his brain doesn't see words the same way mine does. Writing down what he thinks is harder for him. Sometimes he needs an accommodation at school to make things fair. You know how smart he is—he just needs to show people that in a different way sometimes."

I snuck a glance at Eli. He was staring at his sneakers. "I bet you didn't mean to hurt his feelings, Oma. But I think you owe Eli an apology."

Oma turned to Eli, and her face fell. "I apologize, Eli," she said quietly. "You have been a great help to me, and I did not mean to be rude, or hurt your feelings."

"It's okay, Mrs. S.," Eli said. He wasn't smiling anymore, but at least he looked up at us. "I wish I didn't have to have an accommodation either. But they're there to help us."

The ghost nodded. "I see that now. What would you suggest?"

"Well, if the judges can't hear you, HD could tell them what you're saying," Eli said. "Like this girl in our class who can't hear what's going on, so a translator signs everything for her."

"Yes, yes," Oma said, nodding.

"Wait, let's think this through," I said. I could see Eli's point, but I wasn't so sure I wanted to be a ghost's translator at the fair. I had stuff I needed to do—like present my computer. Besides . . . "If they can't see you or hear you, how will they know you're the one

231

who really made the sauerkraut? I mean, what if they give me the prize, just because I'm the only one there they can see? I don't want to wreck your chance to level up."

"Then you will tell them that I am right there, and that they must give the prize to me." Oma folded her ghostly arms and looked stubborn.

I looked at Eli. I was pretty sure that wasn't going to go well.

"Wait," Eli said. "I think I might have an idea." He left the family room. A minute later, he came back with his mom's old camera that can do video—the one he brought so we could make a video of the goats on their obstacle course. "Maybe we can record a video of her."

"We could try it, I guess," I said.

Asad's cartoon ended, and I turned the TV off. He blinked, and looked around. "HEY, ELI!" he shouted at the top of his lungs. "Want to play checkers?"

"HI, ASAD!" Eli shouted right back. "Not right now—I need to help HD with an experiment."

"I will play with you," the ghost told Asad, floating over to take her place at the game table.

"Fine, but we're going to record you while you play, Oma," I said.

"Make a video of me! I'm going to be FAMOUS!" Asad shouted.

"Yeah, okay," I told him. "But, Asad, no more yelling."

"OKAY!" Asad yelled.

Honestly, that kid has no sense of his own volume. Mom says it will develop with time. I'm pretty sure she's wrong, though.

"Start it up," I told Eli.

The ghost fluffed out her hair a little. "I'm ready," she told me, with a big, stiff smile.

Eli turned the dial to the little video icon and pressed some camera buttons. "Three . . . two . . . one . . . Here we go!"

"Get ready for TOTAL ANNIHILATION, Oma!" Asad yelled.

"Never!" the ghost told him, still smiling.

Eli held the camera, and I set my watch timer for three minutes. We waited as Oma defeated Asad in, like, ten moves, and then tried to explain how he could do better next time.

When my watch beeped, Eli stopped the camera and brought it over to the table.

We all crowded around the little screen on the back.

I could see Asad's head and the checkerboard—but not the ghost.

"Get ready for TOTAL ANNIHILATION, Oma!" Asad's voice came out of the little camera speaker.

He giggled. "That's me!"

I nodded. But I couldn't hear Oma's response, not even when Eli turned up the volume.

We all watched Asad move his checker. It was weird to see Oma's checker fly through the air without seeing her.

"Your turn." Asad's voice boomed out of the speaker, so loud I jumped.

But the video hadn't recorded the ghost's reply.

Oma was staring at the screen like she hadn't really realized that she was a ghost, until now.

"Turn it off," I told Eli.

Eli stopped the video. "Maybe there's a setting we can change. Something that can make her louder, and visible. I could check the manual."

"You can check, but I don't think it's just a setting," I said.

Asad ran back to the checkerboard. "I'm getting ready for total annihilation again, Oma!"

But the ghost didn't join him. She looked down at her own ghostly hands, and I wondered if they looked solid to her. "What now?" she asked.

"I don't know," I told her. "Maybe you could make a poster?"

"Don't you still have to explain a poster to the judges?" Eli asked.

I shrugged. "Maybe we could put that she needs to do a poster instead of talking as a special accommodation."

Eli examined our forms. "But it says you must be there to present it—"no exceptions." I know she'll be there, but what if the judges can't see her, and they think she wants an exception?"

"No one ever entered the pickling contest with a poster!" the ghost said, frowning.

"Well, what would you suggest instead?" I asked. (That's what Mom says when she wants someone to stop whining and start working, or at least help her figure things out.)

The ghost started to glow a little bit red around the edges. I took a step back.

So did Eli. "Um, Mrs. S., are you feeling okay?"

But she just kept getting redder and redder. Not like when Dad gets embarrassed. Like, Christmas-tree-light red.

"I must win the Pickle Prize!" the ghost roared.

Eli took another step back. "Um, Mrs. S., let's talk about this calmly—"

"I will not be calm!" Her ghostly body was starting to boil a little around the edges, like she was too mad to hold it together. "I have waited too long for this!"

"I know, Oma!" I said. "I'm trying to help you figure this out!"

"I MUST WIN!" the ghost yelled, and it was almost-but-not-quite her scary ghost yell.

Asad's eyes got big. He packed all the checkers he'd set out back in the box and ran upstairs with it.

"It's okay, Asad!" I called up after him.

"Okay!" he yelled. But he didn't come down.

The ghost looked after him. Slowly the red started to fade away. She floated to the bottom of the stairs and looked up after Asad.

I sighed. "Look, we'll keep working on this, okay?"

The ghost tried to go up the stairs, but she couldn't get past the fourth step. She never can.

"Let's go find a poster board," Eli said.

"Yeah, see what you can find," I told him. "I need to check on Asad first."

The ghost touched my sleeve as I passed her. "Please, Hans Dieter—will you tell Asad that I am sorry?"

She looked like she really meant it. I sighed. "I'll ask him if he'll come down, so you can tell him yourself," I said, heading up the stairs.

22

After Oma apologized and promised Asad she wouldn't yell anymore, he went off to camp with Dad, and Eli and I decided to take the goats to Uncle Gregor's to make our video of the GOAT Obstacle Course. Rodgers still didn't see why he couldn't focus on knocking Hammerstein off the balance beam instead of walking across it, and Hammerstein chewed on the Hula Hoop, so we had to duct-tape it back together. But overall, it went pretty well.

Since we were there, I decided to fill up Uncle Gregor's recycling with old magazines and papers and wheel it out to the curb while Eli practiced his latest solo.

When I came back inside, I showed him what I'd found. It was an old certificate with fancy type. "Know what this reminds me of?"

Eli grinned. "The World's Best Hay-Loader certificate I made you!"

I nodded. When Eli won a prize at last year's science fair, and I didn't, he decided it wasn't fair that I couldn't show my hay-loader off properly in the gym, but the science judges didn't really want to discuss that any further. So he made me his own prize. It wasn't as good as the real thing, and I'm still going to beat him next year. But I felt better knowing that someone knew what I could do, and respected it.

"I still have it," I told him. "It gave me an idea too.... Want to head over to the library? I need to ask Harry about something."

That night, after dinner, we had a special viewing of the GOAT Obstacle Course video. My parents laughed so hard I thought they might hurt themselves, and even Oma cheered. Asad said it would have been way better if he was in it too, so we should do another one.

Then Oma told us she'd made something special for dessert.

Eli and I shut our eyes and tried to guess what it could be.

"Those almond moon cookies?" I guessed, sniffing hard.

"No, wait, what was that other thing?" Eli said, sniffing too. "The one with the swirls?"

"Wrong!" Oma said, and we opened our eyes. A huge pan of brownies was floating right in front of Asad.

"My favorite!" Asad yelled, and gave Oma a huge hug.

I grinned at her. "Where'd you get the recipe?"

"Mr. Ziedrich's friend Mrs. Alvarez emailed it to me," she said, smiling proudly. "It won a blue ribbon at the fair."

"Mrs. Alvarez gave you her brownie recipe?" I said, surprised. "I thought it was a secret."

"Well, I told her it was a special request from my grandsons—and then I had to send her my Kirschen-kuchen recipe in exchange," Oma said. She looked down at Asad, and smiled. "It was a good trade."

Then it was Asad's turn to tell us about the photo he'd picked for our wall.

"This was me on my birthday," he said. "Right after my brother FINALLY let me use his Mentos tube for the first time, and Diet Coke went STRAIGHT UP EVERYWHERE! Then it went ALL OVER ME!"

We all clapped for him, and he grinned almost as wide as he did in the photo.

I couldn't help but grin too. "Yeah, that was pretty cool. We should probably do it again this summer. Only, this time you should at least try to get out of the way."

"NEVER!" Asad yelled, and did a happy stomping dance, with a lot of punching.

He'd be pretty cute sometimes, if he wasn't my annoying little brother.

"We can have a PARTY for ME and the Mentos and SCIENCE!" Asad went on.

"A science party?" Mom asked as she and Dad started gathering plates.

"Sure!" Eli told her, following them into the kitchen. "Science is awesome! It could be kind of like a science fair, or maybe like the county fair, only the food and the recital and everything would all be science-related. . . ."

"And Mom and Dad and Oma and Eli and Rodgers and Hammerstein and Uncle Gregor and Andre and I guess my brother, HD, could all come . . . ," Asad went on.

"Who is Andre?" Oma asked him.

"Andre is Uncle Gregor's BOYFRIEND!" Asad told her. "He loves science so much they're off doing science RIGHT NOW!"

Oma looked at me, confused.

I hesitated. I was pretty sure this was one of those things that had been different when Oma was alive, and I didn't know if Mom and Dad had talked with her about it or not, or if they'd covered it on the History Channel. But Uncle Gregor was her family too. "Oma, do you know about how some guys fall in love with guys, not girls? Uncle Gregor fell in love with a guy he met when he went back to college. His name is Andre." I went over to the mantel and found the photo from when Uncle Gregor and Andre took us for a special backstage tour of the penguin exhibit at the zoo. Uncle Gregor has his arm around Andre's shoulders, and they're both squinting at the sun and smiling. "This is Uncle Gregor, and that's Andre," I told Oma. "They're off doing research on penguins. They'll be back in September, though."

She took the photo from my hand and studied it for a long time. "I cannot wait to meet them," she said at last. "Does Andre make sauerkraut?"

After that, we were all pretty busy getting everything ready for the fair.

Dad dropped our entry forms off and paid the entry fees for me and Oma, since we'd been working so hard on our projects.

Mr. Z. walked me through putting a free open-source operating system and some basic software on my computer, like a word processor and a game I bought, so I could show the judges that it did something. (It's going to be a while before I save up enough money for all the software I want. But like Mr. Z. said, this is a start.)

Eli practiced two solos until they were both nearly perfect, even when the goats came over to see what he was doing. He'll pick which one he wants to do once he's up on stage doing his thing. Eli likes some spontaneity in his performances.

Mr. Z. signed Rodgers and Hammerstein up for the fair, but he decided not to enter the goat-and-owner look-alike contest this year, so we didn't have to help him make costumes. We had to make a few repairs to Eli's costume after an incident with Asad and a football and the goats, though.

Eli and I helped Oma make a really nice poster, and she seemed okay with it now. We helped her write out what she wanted to say on index cards too, to hold up if the judges had questions about her sauerkraut.

I made some cards about my computer build too, and practiced a few times during our kaffeeklatsches. Mr. Z. said I covered everything perfectly.

And Mom let me use her email account to let everyone know when my presentation was scheduled, in case they wanted to come by. Every single one of them said they'd be there.

It was all coming together, just like I wanted it to.

23

On the morning of our fair day, Mom picked her giant kohlrabi and left early to help her farmers set up their vegetables. She dropped Asad off at his friend Liya's house on her way, so he wouldn't get underfoot.

Then Eleanora and Mr. Z. came by to pick up Rodgers and Hammerstein and wish us luck.

"Are you sure you don't want to enter them in the obstacle course?" Eli asked. "They get almost halfway through ours now."

Mr. Z. smiled. "This year, we will let someone else win. But next year . . ."

Total annihilation, Oma wrote, nodding.

After they left, Eli and I got kind of fidgety too, especially with Oma asking if it was time yet every five minutes. So it wasn't that long before Dad suggested we start packing things up. Eli's tap performance wasn't until five, but Oma and I had to have our entries there by nine a.m., even though they wouldn't start judging our categories until ten.

Dad helped me pack the jar of sauerkraut and the poster and my computer and peripherals into the restored 1958 Chevy Impala he was entering this year, and buckle Oma's empty crock into the backseat with us.

When we walked into the gym, I saw a sign on the table by my spot: HD SCHENK, HOMEBUILT COMPUTER. I got a feeling in my stomach, like butterflies that could turn into fireworks, or something magic. Like maybe people would look at me and realize that there was a whole part of me they'd never recognized before, and that what they saw impressed them.

"Are you sure you're going to be okay setting everything up yourselves?" Dad asked, putting his box down.

I nodded. "Yeah, pickles are across the gym, so we'll help Oma get set up too. We just have to get our badges, and make everything look good, and wait for the judges to come around at ten."

"I'm over in the garage if you need anything," he said, squeezing my shoulder. "See you at ten. You do know how proud we are of you, right?"

I felt a butterfly twitch and take off as I nodded. "See you then."

I didn't think it was a good idea to leave Oma by herself, so Eli and I brought her crock along when we went to the table to get our badges.

"Name?" said the white guy sitting at the table, when it was our turn. He smiled at Eli, but he gave me a look like he didn't really want to help me at all. Eli stopped smiling and folded his arms.

"Mrs. Marietta Schenk would like me to pick up her badge, please," I said very politely, setting the crock down.

The guy frowned. "Mrs. Schenk must be present at the time of judging."

I nodded. "She knows. We're helping her get set up."

He gave the pickling crock a look. "There's not much space on the pickle table," he said. "Are you sure she needs that?"

"Yeah, I'm sure," I told him. "Can we please pick up Mrs. Schenk's badge for her?" My stomach was feeling bad-sick now, not butterfly-strange.

The guy shook his head. "She's going to have to sign for that herself."

"Are you saying that because HD's Black?" Eli asked. "Because you let that white lady before us pick up her kid's badge. Maybe you should think harder about what's going into your decisions, because my mom says that is not fair and not okay."

Oma's eyes narrowed. "I will handle this man myself." She grabbed the pen right out of his hand, and signed the form on his clipboard.

"What the—" The guy flinched. He stared at the badges moving in his box. When Oma found hers and pulled it out, not being too careful about how close she got it to his face either, he got to his feet and backed away. Then he turned and ran.

"Come on," I told Eli and Oma, and grabbed the crock. I didn't know when that guy was going to come back, but I didn't want to be there when he did.

That guy was right about one thing, though: There wasn't much room for pickles. So, Oma moved the other people's signs over a little bit to make her spot big enough for her poster and her crock.

"We never got our badges," Eli reminded me. "We're not supposed to be in here without them."

"Maybe we should wait awhile," I said.

Eli went and stuck his head out the gym door. "Don't worry, that guy is still gone." He headed out.

"We'll be back in a minute, okay?" I told Oma, hurrying after him. Maybe nobody would notice her badge floating around the other pickle entries.

When we got there, you know who'd taken that guy's place? Ms. Stevermer!

"Nice to see you," I said. "Can we get our badges? We already got Oma's, but we had to leave before we got ours."

Ms. Stevermer handed over her clipboard and pen. "Yes, I heard about that. So sorry I wasn't here to help."

"That's okay," I told her as she showed us where to sign. "Oma's not that patient, but she's pretty good at managing."

Ms. Stevermer handed us our badges. Eli's said TAP RECITAL on it. Mine said TECHNOLOGY ENTRY.

We put them on and gave each other a high five. We were official now.

"Please tell Mrs. Schenk I wish her the best of luck with her entry," Ms. Stevermer said. "And of course, I'll be thinking of you two as well—though you hardly need luck, with all the work you've put in!"

When we got back to the gym, Oma floated right over, still holding her badge. "HD, come tell me whether the sauerkraut jar looks better on the right side of the crock or the left.... Also, I think the bow on the jar could be bigger. Those pickled beets have a bigger bow."

I glanced at my watch. Nine-thirty. "Look, Oma, I'll come help you in a minute, but I really need to set

my entry up first. I have to be ready at ten too, remember?"

Oma blinked, and looked across the gym at my spot. "I see."

"I can help you, though," Eli told her, practicing his second solo grand finale. He slid to a stop right in front of her entry.

"Thanks," I told him, and left before Oma could argue.

It felt good to set my computer up in the spot with my name. I plugged the monitor into the computer, and connected the keyboard and mouse up again. I plugged the power strip I'd brought into the outlet, and plugged everything else into the power strip. Then I double-checked that all the connectors were secure. I arranged the keyboard in front of the monitor so they lined up neatly, put the Black Panther mouse pad that Dad got for me under the mouse, and stacked up my index cards. Everything was ready.

I checked my watch: nine-forty. I hurried across the gym to see how Eli and the ghost were doing.

"See, none of the other pickling people have any visual aids at all!" Eli was telling the ghost. "You're going to do great, Mrs. S."

"Let me get my pencil." The ghost tried to clip her badge to her pajamas. It fell right through her and landed on the gym floor. She looked up at me. "HD, I need an accommodation for my badge."

It took us a minute to find some supplies, but by nine-fifty I'd made a pretty good badge holder for my great-great-grandma out of a broken shoelace and a paper clip.

The ghost put it over her arm and wore it like a purse. It didn't fall through her shoulder. "How do I look?" She did a little ghostly twirl.

"Very, uh, like a master pickler," I told her, smiling.

Eli was staring at her badge holder. "How is that working?"

I shrugged. "Maybe her pajamas can't handle as much weight as she can?"

"We're going to need to design a new experiment. . . ." Eli trailed off. "Hey, Mrs. S.? You're going to say bye to us before you leave, right?"

"What do you mean?" Oma asked, frowning.

"You know, when you win the fair and go to the next level," Eli said. "Should we say bye now, just in case? Or will you come over to clap for HD's computer before you disappear forever?"

I swallowed. I'd been working so hard to get things ready for this day, I forgot that this could be it. "You're going to stay for the award ceremony tonight, though—right, Oma?"

"I don't know," she said softly. She looked at me, and then down at her stack of index cards. "Perhaps I will not win after all."

I looked out across the gym at my computer. It was still really important to me. But Oma's sauerkraut was important to her too. What if she missed her chance because they couldn't hear her? Maybe I could help Oma with her presentation and still do mine. . . . After all, the judges couldn't visit all the entries at once.

"I have an idea," I said. "Eli, can you come help me talk to Ms. Stevermer again for a minute? Don't go anywhere yet, Oma—we'll be right back."

We ran back to the registration table. "We think Oma might need my help presenting her sauerkraut," I told Ms. Stevermer. "We helped her make a poster, but the judges probably can't hear her, so I might need to tell them what she says."

"As an accommodation," Eli added.

Ms. Stevermer thought about that for a minute. "Well, I've never seen anything about ghosts not being allowed to enter the fair, so let's proceed as we would for anyone else who was entering. Would you say she's missing her vocal cords and larynx?"

Eli and I nodded. "Yeah, she's missing her whole body," I said.

"If an entrant needed an accommodation due to a missing body part, we would of course accommodate her, and I don't see why a missing body would be any different," Ms. Stevermer said. "You'll only be telling the judges what she said, correct? And she'll need to sign for herself."

I nodded. "Yeah, it's her presentation."

"And you know she can write just fine," Eli said.

Ms. Stevermer nodded, and wrote a note on a piece of scratch paper. "Have her sign this. It will let the judges know you've been approved to help her."

"Thanks," I told her, taking the note. We hurried back to the gym.

"Okay, so here's the new plan," I told Oma. "If you sign this note, I can help you out by telling the judges what you're saying."

Oma straightened up and smiled. "Wonderful!" She picked up her pencil and signed the note.

"A group of judges will be coming in any moment now," I told the ghost. "If they start with the technology side of the gym, I'm going to go present my computer first, and then come back and help you. If they start with this side—"

"You will help me explain how I made my sauerkraut first," the ghost said, nodding. "Thank you, Hans Dieter."

The ghost wrapped her arms around me, and I hugged her back. When I opened my eyes, I saw some lady look at me, then look away fast. But you know what? I didn't really care. Just because she couldn't see everything in the world around her didn't mean I had to do anything differently. Sometimes you have to do what's important to you, no matter what anybody else thinks.

"And if they have any questions, I'll help you answer them, before I go present my computer," I said. "But, try to stick around long enough to say goodbye to everyone, okay? I mean, I know you're probably impatient to move on, but . . . We're going to miss you."

Eli grabbed my arm. "We have a problem," he said. "Look."

Two different groups of judges had arrived, instead of the one group we'd planned for. One group had clipboards and big buttons with canning jars on them, and they were moving toward the first pickle entry. Another had buttons that said STEM, and they were moving toward the first technology entry.

"We can still make this work," Eli said. "Somehow."

Eight entries before Oma's. Nine before mine. There wouldn't be time to do one, then the other.

"I could, uh, create a distraction!" Eli said. "Like, maybe a musical number?"

I'd spent so long getting ready for this day, picturing it in my mind. My computer was waiting for me, right across the gym. All I had to do was turn it on and tell everyone how I built it. For just a minute, I let myself imagine once more how it would be, me explaining how I built my computer, and my parents, Eli, Mr. Z., Harry, Grace, Rose, Mei, and Ms. Stevermer, all nodding along, appreciating what I had done.

But all those people know it's important to help someone out when they need it. Every one of them had helped me out, one time or another.

I imagined myself looking up over all those people's smiles and seeing Oma disappear, without saying goodbye.

I wanted to show everyone I was a maker. But those people already knew that, really. Now I needed to be someone who helps people out too.

I turned my back on the computer that I built, and I told Oma, "Okay. Let's get ready for the judges."

"Ready!" she said, clutching her pencil. She watched the pickling judges coming slowly down the line.

"Wait, what? Are you sure, HD?" Eli asked. "You don't have to do this. I could help her for you, instead."

"Thanks," I told him. "But she's my oma, and I want to be here, in case it's time to say goodbye. Just—

would you keep an eye out for my parents and Mr. Z., and let them know what's going on?"

"Sure thing." Eli hesitated. "I'm really sorry, HD."

I shrugged. It was okay, kind of. But I didn't feel like talking about it anymore. Not when I could see my mom walking up to my computer, looking around for me.

Eli headed across the gym, and I glanced at Oma. She was staring over at my computer.

Slowly she set her pencil down on the entry table. "HD, you do not have to help me," she said, her voice quiet. "You belong there, with the project you worked so hard on, and with your family, and your friends."

"It's okay, Oma," I said. I wiped my hands on my jeans, and watched the judges come closer. "You've waited a long time for this, and you're my family too. I don't want you to be by yourself when it's time for you to move on. I guess I can wait another year."

"Thank you," she said, and her voice was very small, even for a ghost.

And then the judges with the canning-jar buttons were there. "Mrs. Schenk?" one asked, looking around.

I straightened my shoulders. "I'm doing the oral presentation for Mrs. Schenk," I told them. "As an accommodation. We have a note, from Ms. Stevermer."

I handed over the note, and they crowded around to read it.

"This is highly irregular," one of the judges hissed.

Another nodded thoughtfully. "It's never happened before, but everything seems to be in order. On what grounds would you disqualify the entry?"

"On the grounds that it's obviously a ridiculous hoax!" the first judge answered.

Oma didn't like that. *Hans Dieter is my accommodation, and I am not a hoax,* she wrote on a spare card. She held it up before I could stop her.

That was it for the first judge; she took three steps back, then walk-ran out of the gym, muttering.

The second judge snorted. "Would anyone else like to disqualify themselves from their duties as judge?" She raised her pencil up above her clipboard, like it was a race, or a dare.

The other two judges stopped staring, and shook their heads. One kept glancing around, though, like he was trying to figure out if he was on camera, or how the special effects worked.

Then Oma started talking, so I told them what she said while she held up her cards.

"Sauerkraut is made from cabbages," I told them. "It's a traditional German food that means 'sour cabbage,' and that is exactly what it is. Sauerkraut gets its sour flavor when it's fermented, not from vinegar, so it takes time to make. Mrs. Schenk made this sauerkraut from her special recipe, using her pickling crock."

But I sliced the cabbage in the food processor, not with the kraut cutter, the ghost wrote in big letters. *That is a very good invention.*

Across the gym, I caught a glimpse of the other judges asking questions about the crystal radio two entries before my computer. But I didn't stop talking.

"In this country, as in Germany, sauerkraut helped people survive over the winter, and not get sick from not having any vegetables. Like scurvy. You could get scurvy even if you weren't a pirate, if you didn't have any vegetables."

"Young man—er, Mrs. Schenk's representative—please provide more details about her recipe," one of the judges said.

The STEM judges moved on to the Lego robot right before my computer. I saw my dad run in, stop, look around, and say something to my mom.

I took a deep breath, and I focused on what I was doing.

"For this sauerkraut, we used five heads of cabbage, sprinkled with salt," Oma told the judges, so I told them too.

"How much salt?" asked the judge taking notes.

"Enough," Oma said.

"Come on, Oma, you remember—we weighed it and wrote it down!" I whispered.

The ghost sighed. "Very well, but the weight is not as important as whether there is enough brine after you pound the cabbage. We used five and one quarter ounces of salt, young lady. And for my special ingredient, three tablespoons of juniper berries."

I told the judge what Oma said.

She nodded, and the rest of the judges examined the jar and made notes.

"Is there anything else we should know about your recipe, to conclude your presentation?" a different judge asked.

I looked up to see if Oma wanted to add anything else.

She wasn't there.

For a minute, I just stared at the space where she'd been. Had she leveled up before I even finished the presentation? She wouldn't disappear without saying goodbye when I was right there helping her out, would she?

Then I realized the pickling crock lid was missing.

And then I heard Eli's voice over the crowd. "You have to push the monitor button too, Mrs. S."

I looked up, and caught a glimpse of the ghost floating over my keyboard in front of a group of judges.

She handed the pickling crock lid to Eli, and pushed the monitor button.

"Mrs. Schenk?" the judge asked again.

I pulled myself together. "Uh, no, that's all she wants to say about her sauerkraut, thanks," I told the judge.

"Then you are free to go enjoy the fair, young man," the judge said, and went back to examining Oma's sauerkraut and making notes with the others.

So I tore across the gym to my computer. A document was open on my screen, and Oma was typing.

YOUR ATTENTION PLEASE: I AM PROVIDING AN ACCOMMODATION FOR HANS DIETER SCHENK, WHO WILL BE HERE AS SOON AS HE FINISHES HELPING HIS GRANDMOTHER. THIS IS THE COMPUTER HE BUILT. HE IS A FINE YOUNG MAN, AND SHOULD NOT BE PENALIZED FOR HELPING PEOPLE.

"I'm here now," I told the judges, breathing hard. "Thanks, Oma." I took the lid from Eli. Maybe everyone would just decide they hadn't seen the keyboard moving all by itself.

"Did you program that script too?" one of the judges asked, staring at the screen.

"Uh . . . I had some help," I told her, and she made a note.

The other judges seemed to relax after that. I guess they were more comfortable with technology than they were with ghosts.

"Was the CPU preinstalled on the motherboard when you bought it?" another judge asked.

"Nah, I bought them separately and installed it myself," I told the judge. "I installed the CPU fan too, and the memory, and everything. And the case, the motherboard, the monitor, the keyboard, and the mouse were all used, so this demonstrates how you shouldn't just throw useful stuff away."

Rose and Mei and Grace were nodding.

"Is there anything else we should know about your computer?" one of the judges asked.

"As a former engineer, I consulted on this project, and I feel you should know that this young man earned the money himself and did the entire build on his own," Mr. Z. told the judges.

"And as a former information technology specialist for the US Army, I'd like to say he researched his options carefully, modified his plan as necessary, and did an outstanding job of it," Grace added.

I felt the smile on my face grow bigger and bigger.

"This is a far more complex project than any we teach in the library's makerspace," Harry added. "I hope you're taking that into consideration."

"Yes, we will keep all of that in mind as we make our decision," one of the judges said.

Mrs. Alvarez gave him a look. "As the winner of fourteen blue ribbons for baking, I do not want to hear about anyone losing any points because he was helping his grandmother. Is this fair about the community, or not?"

HEAR, HEAR, Oma typed.

The judge who'd asked me about programming gave the screen a hard look, and made a note. Then they all moved on to the next entry.

My mom gave me a big hug. "I'm so proud of you," she whispered.

Dad was grinning. "Seems like you've impressed a lot of people, whether you win or not, buddy."

When Mom let me go, I had to look at my shoes for a minute. Not from being sad, though. From being happy, and proud, and feeling kind of like I might cry from all those feelings wanting to get out any way they could. Which was not what I wanted to do while everybody was looking at me. "Thanks," I said.

"One of the judges said they should disqualify you for not being present, but I told them all about how it was a reasonable accommodation," Eli told me. "And then I kept arguing until you got here. I bet Mom will give me a Top Family Negotiator bonus when she hears about it!"

"Thanks, Eli," I said. It kind of felt like all the butterflies in my stomach were exploding at once. Or maybe that's what it feels like when caterpillars come out of cocoons. I looked up at my great-great-grandma, who was just floating there, letting me have my moment without saying a word. "Thanks, Oma."

Before we moved on, I asked the kid with the Lego robot to take a picture for us. She had to back way up across the room so she could fit us all in: Mom and Dad, Mr. Z. and Mrs. Alvarez and Ms. Stevermer,

Grace and Harry, Rose and Mei, and at the middle of it all, me and Eli, and my computer.

If you look carefully, you can see a badge on a shoelace floating above my dad's shoulder, and above my head too.

Yeah, I know exactly what my first photo on the wall is going to be. Just as soon as I draw the rest of Oma in.

I don't really remember the rest of the fair. I know we watched the goat obstacle course competition and made some notes for what to build next, and went on the Tilt-A-Whirl (except not Oma, who didn't like whirling), and the Ferris wheel (except not Mr. Z., who knows too much about possible points of failure to get on one of those things), and Eli won a cake in the cakewalk, and we all ate it with some forks Mrs. Alvarez had in her purse, along with Harry's extra coconut shortbread. We had our picture taken with Mom's giant kohlrabi, and in Dad's Impala, and in the back of Frank's daughter's cool old Dodge truck.

Eli's mom got back from her trip in time for his recital, and it went great. He got to do both his solos twice, because one of the other skyscrapers ran into the dancer next to her, who fell over and hit the one next to her, and they all went down like dominos. Eli was the only one still standing, because he was paying attention to his surroundings for once and got out of the way in time. So Ms. Izdebski shouted, "Take it away, Eli!" and went to help everyone else get up, and he did. He said all that practice avoiding sneak attacks from Rodgers and Hammerstein and Asad really helped. And Asad got to yell "GO, ELI! YOU'RE KILLING IT, MAN!" as loud as he possibly could and no one told him to be quiet for once.

Eli loved the squirting flower I made him. Now Asad wants one too.

Oma volunteered me to bring her crock over to Ms. Stevermer's house sometime so she could take

a look at another crock Ms. Stevermer had, and try to help her figure out if anybody was home. Harry offered to teach me how to make his coconut short-bread, and Oma asked if I'd teach her, then, too. And when Grace asked me what I was thinking about for my entry next year, I told her my plan—after I swore her to secrecy.

She thought it was a great idea. She even asked if she could be my project consultant.

I can't wait to get started.

And then it was time for the awards ceremony.

25

Dad's Impala won a second-place ribbon, but the rest of us didn't win anything this year. I got beat by the Lego robot (which, I have to say, really was pretty cool), and Mom's kohlrabi got beat by someone's tomato. Oma's sauerkraut didn't even get an honorable mention.

I wasn't as upset as I thought I'd be, though. I guess it was hard to be all that disappointed when everyone I cared about kept telling me how impressed they were. One of the judges wrote, *Great work! I'll be looking for your entry next year.*

But I was worried about Oma. "I'm sorry," I told her. "I thought we did a good job."

"It was perfect," Oma told me. She didn't turn red and yell, or even seem that upset. She examined June Lee's blue ribbon. "What is kimchi?"

I shrugged. "It's a kind of Korean pickle. I think it might be spicy," I told her.

"We will find out what it is, and then we will make it," Oma said. She floated over so she could read the judges' notes.

"Maybe she's not ready to level up yet after all," Eli said. "Maybe she wants to make some more sauerkraut first. We can try again next year, though."

I watched as Asad ran over and gave the ghost a big hug. "Maybe," I said. "Or maybe winning the prize isn't her Grand Purpose after all. Maybe she just wants to spend some time with her family." Either way, she didn't seem to be going anywhere right away.

That was fine with me.

We stayed all the way till closing time, past when Liya got off the Tilt-A-Whirl and threw up a whole funnel cake and her mom took her home, past when Eli's mom fell asleep in the middle of the high school kids' marching-band contest because of jet lag, and Mom told her to go home and get some rest, we'd drop Eli off later.

We helped Mei wrap her latest junk creation up in old blankets and shove it into her trailer, and told her we couldn't wait to see what she made for next year's art competition. Rose said she didn't really see how you can top a ten-foot-tall welded junk dragon with hubcaps for eyes and old fire pokers for claws, even if Mei hadn't had time to make it breathe fire like we'd suggested. But if anyone can, it's Mei.

But finally, the fair people wanted to go home, and that meant we had to leave too. So Eli and my parents and Mr. Z. helped me carry everything over to where our cars were parked while Asad ran around playing tag with Oma and teasing the goats and not being very helpful at all. Dad opened the Impala's enormous trunk, and after a few tries, we fit everything inside.

I picked up the box I'd taken out, and walked around to the hood, where the ghost was tickling Asad.

"Oma, I'm sorry you didn't win today," I told her. "But I want you to know that we think you're the best, no matter what the judges decided."

I set the box down on the hood and took off the lid. "We made this for you." I pulled out the brand-new

Schenk Family Pickle Prize. It was only plastic, but it was shaped like a fancy trophy cup with handles, and it said MRS. MARIETTA SCHENK, 1ST PLACE on the bottom. Harry taught me how to design and 3-D-print it in the makerspace, and Mr. Z. and Dad helped me figure out which gold paint to use on the plastic.

I handed it to Oma. "I hereby award you first place in the Schenk Family Pickle Contest!"

"Oh, Hans Dieter!" she said, swooping down to hug me.

"Just don't get so happy you go anywhere yet," I said. "There's more."

"These beautiful flowers are for you, Oma!" Asad yelled, smacking her in the stomach with the corsage he picked out. It was the brightest one in the store, orange and purple and red and yellow, all at once, and it was a little wilty, even with that tube of water that comes with it. But Oma said she loved it anyway. (It did dress up her pajamas.)

I helped her pin it onto her badge holder so she could wear it without it falling through her body and getting dirty.

"We really need to set up a new experiment to figure out how she's holding that up," Eli told me.

I nodded. "Yeah, we'll put it on the list."

Then it was Mom's turn. "I don't know if this is exactly what you were thinking of when you told me about the parade," she said, kind of hesitantly. "But this was my grandmother's best church hat. It's very special to me. I would be honored if you would wear it in our Schenk Family Parade." She took out a hat covered in flowers and ribbons and stuff.

By now, Oma was crying her blue-white streaks again, but she was smiling too. She didn't say anything, just swooped down, took the hat out of Mom's hands, and gave Mom a big hug.

"She gave you a hug, Mom," I said. "I think she likes it."

Mom touched her shoulder where Oma had hugged her. "I think I felt that," she said wonderingly.

We watched as the ghost put Mom's grandmom's hat on. She had to kind of hold it up with one hand, but at least she didn't let it fall through her head.

"It looks good on you," I told her, and the ghost smiled.

"Now, I'm not the mayor," Dad said, holding out his arm. "But, Oma, would you do me the honor of riding in my award-winning car in the Schenk Family Parade?"

"It would be my honor," the ghost said, smiling, and put her ghostly hand on his arm.

I smiled. "She says let's do this."

"Hang on a minute here," Mom said. "We have another person we need to honor first." She brought her hands out from behind her back, and I saw that she was holding a messenger bag. It was tan and had a cool old-school style to it. On the flap, it said MAKER TOOLKIT in dark-brown letters.

I swallowed. I didn't know what to say.

"Wow!" Eli said. "HD, that is awesome!"

Dad came around to stand next to Mom. "HD, we want you to know how proud we are of everything you've done. Maybe those judges have no idea what it takes to build a computer. But we saw how hard you worked to earn that money, and how you planned your project out and made it happen. We want you to know that, in our eyes, you won first place before we even got here." He shook his head and smiled. "Now that you're taking on projects we've never tried, we want to give you the tools you might need. So Mr. Ziedrich and Grace and Harry gave us a few ideas, and . . . Well, we hope you like them."

Mom walked forward. She slung the bag around my head and my arm, like she was Princess Leia giving me a medal. Then she kissed my forehead. "You had a tough call to make today," she said. "How did I get such a smart, handsome, helpful young man for a son, anyway?"

I shrugged. I couldn't stop grinning. "Just lucky, I guess."

Mom rolled her eyes. "Mmmm-hmmmm, as if!"

"I want one too!" Asad yelled, tugging at my bag.

Mom shook her head. "That is a special gift that HD earned with his hard work."

I looked inside. There was an electric screwdriver and bits, some cool safety goggles, a whole bunch of different kinds of glue, some pliers, a measuring tape, some gloves, a book on making electronics projects, and a new maker's notebook with a cool mechanical pencil. And there was Mr. Z.'s computer tool kit too. "Maybe when you're my age, if you work hard, you'll get something this cool," I told him.

Oma floated over to give me a hug. "Thank you for everything, Hans Dieter," she told me. Then she looked at Asad's face. "Now then, since I am the Pickle Queen, I will need a knight to wave in my parade," she told him.

"OKAY!" Asad yelled, suddenly happy again.

After Mr. Z. took a picture of us all, he and Rodgers and Hammerstein got into Eleanora's van, and Dad buckled Oma's crock up in the front seat while Eli and I sat in the back. Mom and Asad and Eleanora and Mr. Z. drove behind us, to make it a real parade.

"HEY, PEOPLE, IT'S TIME TO WAVE!" Asad shouted out the window as Dad started the Impala.

Everyone in the parking lot waved as we went past, because even though they couldn't see Oma waving, they could see us (and they could definitely hear Asad).

And as we drove away, off to the park where we

could put our blankets on the grass and watch the fireworks light up the sky, I heard a middle school guy tell his friend, "That kid? That's HD Schenk. He makes computers for ghosts. I saw one typing on it earlier and everything."

"Whoa," said his friend, eyes wide.

Eli elbowed me. "Uh, HD? I really think it might be an age thing. We'd better design that experiment and find out who else can see her."

"Yeah, we'll put it on the list," I said. I met those kids' eyes and gave them the nod.

So that's how people thought of me now . . . a maker who builds computers for ghosts.

Uh-huh.

I could live with that.

At least, until next year's fair.

Because my next project? Well, let me just tell you this: it's going to be even better.

ACKNOWLEDGMENTS

Thank you to Sundee Frazier, Nita Tyndall, Aarene Storms, Jim Beidle, Eric Lakin, Ryan, Danny, and Ansel Idryo, Sarah Keliher, Jan and Jenny Waggoner, Chiemi Davis, Kikora Dorsey, Luisa Weiss's *Classic German Baking*, Linda Ziedrich's *The Joy of Pickling*, the friendly bakers at Kaffeeklatsch, New Moon Farm's Goatalympics, the writers of Black Nerd Problems, Artie Bennett, Iris Broudy, Alison Kolani, Marianne Cohen, Jake Eldred, and everyone who helped me make this book richer, deeper, and better.

Thank you to Melissa Koosmann, Liz Wong, Jen Adam, Edith Hope Bishop, Brenna Shanks, Marin Younker, Mike Denton, Sarah Hunt, Alison Weatherby, Courtney Gould, Gillian Allen, Jenny Scott Tynes, and my Emerald City Literary Agency and SCBWI Western Washington friends and colleagues, who keep me writing. Special thanks to Caroline Stevermer, who, upon hearing that a haunted pickling crock popped up in my story, really did declare that all pickling crocks are haunted, and to Kim Baker, whose *Pickle: The (Formerly) Anonymous Prank Club of Fountain Point Middle School* inspired me.

Thank you to all who share my stories with readers: Josh Redlich, Elena Meuse, Shaughnessy Miller, Deanna Meyerhoff,

Lisa Nadel, Kristin Schulz, Lisa McClatchy, Adrienne Waintraub, Rene Holderman, Niki Marion, Sam Kaas, Suzanne Perry, Christy McDanold, Rene Kirkpatrick, Grace Rajendran, Tegan Tigani, Jenny Cole, Annie Carl, Michelle Bear, Mary Kay Sneeringer, Holly Myers, Karen Maeda Allman, Dan and Tina Ullom, Chris Jarmick, Lillian Welch, Cecilia Cackley, Alene Moroni, Stephanie Chase, Anna Mickelsen, Jenny Craig, Joy Feldman, Kiera Parrott, Monica Edinger, Kit Ballenger, Amber Bauer, and all the amazing booksellers, teachers, bloggers, reviewers, and librarians who've made sharing a love of reading their life's work.

Thank you to Mandy Hubbard and Nancy Siscoe, who believed in this book from the beginning, to Marisa DiNovis and Garrett Alwert, who kept us all afloat, and to Bob Bianchini and Trish Parcell, who put everything together so beautifully.

Thank you to Paul Davey, who brought HD and his story to life with such magic and grace.

Stories don't grow in vacuums. Thank you to all the makers, geeks, picklers, bakers, junkyard aficionados, goat caretakers, tap dancers, mechanics, farmers, soldiers, engineers, scientists, curious people, and readers who make my world such an interesting place. Special thanks to those who trusted me with their names and their personal explorations of family and heritage: you gave this book its heart.

Thank you to my family and friends, who believe in making stuff, testing things, helping people, knowing where we came from, and thinking about who we want to be. I love you guys.